GAZE:

A Novel

by Stuart Suskind

ISBN 13: 978-1-944662-75-2

Cover Design by Kelly Nielsen, Studio 92 © 2022 (www.studio92.us)

Dedication

This book is lovingly dedicated to my wife Cherry without whose assistance I could never undertake a project like this.

Table of Contents

Stuart Suskind

Acknowledgments

As far back as I can remember, my mother's eyes always told me a story, sometimes sad, sometimes very distant, sometimes very happy, but I could always count on that special look of caring and love that was uniquely hers.

About the Author

Stuart Suskind is a retired patent agent and research chemist. He lives in Leland North Carolina outside of Wilmington. For fun he hits a few tennis balls and plays classical clarinet. His email address is:

stuartsuskind2020@gmail.com

Chapter 1

The main campus of the university was comprised of a well-kept grass quadrangle surrounded by brick red, asymmetric, federal-style buildings that housed the various departments in the sciences and arts. A walking path of concrete paver blocks led down from the rear of the law school into a pine forest. Paths from the other buildings intersected leading to one wider walkway with benches and tables lining it. This was a favorite place for students to congregate between classes for studies, lunch, and socializing.

The warm, breezy September sunshine was the perfect accompaniment to the chatter about this totally new experience and a welcome break from the dull classroom. The morning's lecture on legal brief writing seemed to be the most popular topic. Some of the students had worked for law firms and were familiar with the writing styles of experienced attorneys, who did not necessarily follow the accepted formats and preferred to add a twist of creative thinking into their writing.

This morning the lecturing professor had given an explanation with examples of the IRAC method of legal writing and reasoning. In this simple formula, "I" stood for the issue or question at hand, "R" for the appropriate rule or law, "A" for the application of the facts of the case, and "C" for conclusion. The formula was more than an outline for writing; it was a guideline for proper legal thinking taught to students from the very beginning. The professor expounded upon the field of law, the profession these students hoped to be able to practice upon graduation, although for many just the thought of getting a job remained uppermost in their minds since they had families to support and had to repay the money they borrowed to get their degree.

Aaron was reminded of his own doubts about going to law school. He believed that politics, following in his father's footsteps, was the right career path for him. Knowing the law and how it was written would prove vital to anyone who wanted to make a future in the field. But he realized it took more than understanding of the law to find success in politics. His father's knowledge of people was critical to his success. Aaron resolved that, starting today, he would begin his legal career by making communication his highest priority, becoming a good listener and an observer of facial expressions.

Aaron sat down at one of the tables and mentally reviewed the elements required for good legal writing and reasoning. With politics as his ultimate career goal, he would remember the IRAC formula. He listened to some of the students chatting about the upcoming coursework, about the anticipated long homework assignments, and, of course, exams as the keys to making good grades.

As Aaron observed his surroundings, he noticed a young woman sitting alone, not sharing in the laughter and noise. She seemed pensive and even a little concerned. Her hair was black and shoulder length and her eyes spoke of deeper thoughts. His grandmother had told him many times that the way to learn about somebody was through the expressions of their eyes. People could say almost anything, and some learned to tell lies in a convincing way. But the eyes could give a lie away. Seeing through a lot of talk could be like a puzzle or a riddle. Aaron sometimes found it fun trying to decipher those hidden truths.

"Did this morning's lecture strike any familiar notes with you?" Aaron inquired of this enigmatic young woman.

"No," she said shaking her head. "My undergraduate degree is in library science. I was going to become a librarian." Extending her hand, she added, "Sara Knight, librarian. This is all very new to me."

"Nice to meet you, Sara. I'm Aaron. I have to say law school is a far cry from libraries and librarians."

"Pleased to meet you, Aaron. Yes, a number of people are trying to figure out why I decided to attend law school."

"I would be very interested in hearing that decision process. Anyone in particular influence your thinking?"

"Yes, in fact, there was. It was my father but, of course, he influences all of my decisions, but he does it in such a way that I think *I'm* the one coming up with the ideas and making the decisions. He's a great man with great powers, and he can do that."

She noted the time and gathered her things. "It was lovely to talk with you," she said smiling.

Aaron returned the grin. "We should do this again," he said. "But let's watch the clock a little better or we might be late."

The two of them stood and walked briskly to their next class.

As weeks went by the fall sun continued to warm the campus and outdoor breaks remained popular. Aaron and Sara spent many of those occasions together. They would walk down the pathway and then sit on the bench opposite the stairwell.

One particularly warm afternoon, he took out a bottle of Evian water from his case and started to unscrew the cap.

She reached down and touched the bottle, remarking, "I don't think I've ever seen anyone carrying a bottle of Evian. Isn't that expensive when we have water fountains in every campus building?"

"I just like it," he said.

"How about letting me try it? I want to taste the difference," Sara said.

"You know I've had this bottle to my mouth several times. Let's wipe off the..."

She interrupted, "It's really no different than if we kissed each other, and I know you want to kiss me."

Her eyes gleamed in the sunlight, and the corners of her mouth turned ever so slightly upward. She leaned towards him almost imperceptibly.

He perceived that as an invitation. Extending his free hand, he gently touched her neck and guided her head towards his. Her lips were full and warm. He could tell by the way she kissed that she'd done this many times. He wondered if his experiences could come close to matching hers.

"How did you know I wanted to kiss you?" he said.

"I knew because I have a talent along these lines. Surely you knew that I was a *talented* girl," she said with a flirtatious grin.

He responded, "Yes, I feel you have many talents, and I hope to be able to discover them all."

"We shall see. We shall see. But on the subject of discovering, I'll have you know I was one of the very first among all my friends and relatives to discover the wonders of sushi."

What a great opening, he thought.

"So you're sushi lover? Well, so am I. I know the best sushi restaurant in town. How about joining me for dinner?"

"When did you have in mind?"

"How about Saturday night?"

"Okay, we've got a date," Sara said.

Chapter 2

Aaron's favorite restaurant was packed that Saturday night. Fortunately, the line to get a table was short and after only a few minutes they found a spot. Immediately upon being seated, they grabbed the menu and started to laugh and make fun of each other's pronunciation of Japanese words. He liked the sound of her laughter as it rose from deep inside her chest, which likely meant that she had a good sense of humor.

The waiter stood, pencil in hand, waiting for them. Fortunately, they found a mixture of sushi and sashimi on the menu that was meant for two people. That would make the ordering process easy and so they went for it.

After the waiter left with their order, Aaron kept the conversation flowing.

"So, you're pretty good at predicting people's behavior," he said referring to her insight about his desire to kiss her.

"Well, that example the other day was pretty easy. I could tell by the way you were looking at me. I've seen it with other guys."

"I have a kind of a talent along those lines too," Aaron said. "It involves the eyes. A few years ago, I noticed that when people are excited or angry or really happy and laughing, you can see that emotion in their eyes. Back in my senior year in high school, I had a date with a girl who was talking very excitedly about her plans for college and for her career. She was really animated, and I thought I would try an experiment to see if I could really impress her. Back then, guys were always trying to find a way to impress women."

"When you say, 'back then,' do you mean that guys don't try to impress women now?" she asked smiling.

He grinned at her remark but continued the discussion. He explained that he had the ability to tell a person all about their emotions and that he could read what was important in life by looking into someone's eyes. He had already heard some of the important things in her life, so that part was pretty easy.

"Why don't you try it with me and rely only on what you see in my eyes because you haven't heard that much about my life," she said playfully, inviting him to take a good, hard look at her eyes.

Aaron leaned forward and peered deeply into her eyes. He convincingly moved and bobbed his head about seriously as if keenly searching for a clue. He paused, relaxed for a moment, and then started again, slowly and deliberately gazing into her eyes.

"What's taking you so long?" she asked. "Am I so complicated? Are you're trying to unravel the great mystery?"

Aaron felt his heart racing. As he had done in the past, he searched for words that might be amusing in keeping with the parlor game mood. He struggled to break the silence. He saw something in her eyes that disturbed him, something he had never seen before, and something he could not immediately explain. He felt a sense of panic, of alarm. Searching for an amiable way to end the conversation, he told her that, as expected, he saw that she was inquisitive about what law school and the exams would be like. He lied. He had actually seen something that frightened him.

Chapter 3

Edvin Karlsson was born in 1910 in the traditional paper mill town of Halmstad, Sweden. He was an only child to his parents Greta and Ludwig Karlsson, who were relatively low-paid workers at the mill. Edvin attended public schools and finally took a course in paper technology paid for by the state. He was given the position of trainee in the production department and after two years was promoted to assistant foreman.

Greta and Ludwig maintained an appearance of pride in their son to their friends in this closely-knit, traditional town. But strong emotions lurked behind the surface of this pride. They envied their son's good education and career. They had been given no such advantage and were required to toil laboriously at the lowest level in the mill.

The skill with which they hid their emotions was among their finest talents. The boy appreciated his parents, yet he felt something missing that he could not identify, let alone articulate. He grew up with a kind of vacancy in his feelings towards them. He was bright though and filled this slight sense of emptiness with hard work and solid achievements in the mill.

In 1945, the management of the mill decided to transfer Edvin to their United States affiliate in order to provide technology transfer and generally improve communications between the two sites. Not wanting to stand out as a foreigner, he changed his name to Garland Knight, married a young lady, also of Swedish heritage, and had a daughter Sara in 1950. She had majored in library science but was later persuaded by her father to become a lawyer.

After working in the United States for a few years, Garland Knight became well known in his community through his constant efforts to improve education, roads, sanitation, and anything where he could make suggestions and even provide advances that helped others. While never an official or employee of the community, he could be found in municipal halls several times a month, poking his head wherever he could do some good. And he was welcomed because, as people learned, he could get things done.

Professionally, he had reached the position of director of manufacturing at the Preston Pulp and Paper Corporation. After graduating with a degree in paper engineering, he had worked in almost every department of the Preston company and had gained respect through technical innovations, useful changes in organization, and an inherent ability to lead. He made many contributions to the company's growth through the years.

In his personal life, he was proud of his attractive wife and good-looking, well-dressed daughter, who seemed well behaved and was a pretty good student.

Garland could walk with his head high, proud of where he had arrived in his life, especially considering the fact that his parents had not even finished high school. He was given little money for his education and attained this stage of his life pretty much on his own.

Yet he was troubled. There seemed to be something in the air in his home life that he sensed wasn't quite right. The harder he tried to correct or figure out what was wrong, the more the situation eluded him. He sensed an intangible problem. The best he could discern was that it related mostly to his daughter and to some extent his wife, who seemed to feed the underlying issue in some way. He felt something was *off*, deeply wrong.

Chapter 4

In the days and nights that followed, Aaron found himself engrossed in the study of legal proceedings. He paused over the section on frivolous lawsuits, noting that they were not really serious cases, perhaps only intended to embarrass or to annoy another party.

His thoughts turned to the eye-reading game that he liked to play. It too was frivolous and was meant only for fun. But now he could not forget the expression he thought he saw in Sara's eyes, something he had never seen before and could not understand. But, of course, he had just met her and knew little about her. This game of his only worked when he had enough information about the person's life. Despite the heavy course load they both carried, he determined to learn much more about her and try to solve this mystery.

His mind returned to the many stories he had been told by his grandparents. Filip and Gabriella Seitner were born at the close of the 19th century as Polish citizens living in the Free City of Danzig. Danzig was freed under the Treaty of Versailles in 1920. The city was populated mainly by Germans and native Polish citizens including about 10,000 Jews, who comprised about two percent of the population.

Filip was a physician trained in the prestigious medical school at the University of Vienna. He knew all of the best and most modern treatments and medicines and possessed fine-tuned analytical skills and an easygoing bedside manner, which made him one of the most sought-after physicians in the city. Like most of the Jews of Danzig, he belonged to the great synagogue, and it was there that his medical practice grew through word of mouth. The Seitners held a social position in the temple where they were respected and were often called upon for their leadership.

Gabriella's profession was less well defined, although it was generally understood that she did some kind of counseling. She was loved and respected by those who knew her either as a friend or client. She was a wonderful listener with a sympathetic ear. She often paid visits to members of the congregation who were experiencing some form of emotional upheaval or trouble.

Gabriella had an engaging personality, and she often found herself invited to the home of a woman who was experiencing some difficulty and who wanted a follow-up to the warm and engaging conversation Gabriella regularly shared after a Sabbath service. These home visits soon became weekly sessions with her host gradually pouring out her heart to Aaron's grandmother. Many were in awe of her ability to quickly understand and empathize with other people's feelings.

As Filip and Gabriella began to appreciate each other's professional accomplishments, they started to discuss the approaches that were bringing them such success. Filip had a confident manner and a relaxed and easy way of communicating with his patients. He combined these with his medical education, which he supplemented with constant reading and discussions with other doctors to learn the most modern and effective methods of understanding and curing disease.

Gabriella had a harder time explaining her success since there was no official profession of marriage counseling or personal therapy in the suburbs of Danzig at that time.

"What kinds of conversations do you have with women who eventually become your patients?" Filip asked her in the late evening as they prepared to go to bed.

"It varies quite a bit; it depends on what I see in a particular person."

"I'm not sure what you mean by what you *see* in a person," her husband replied.

"I can read their hopes, disappointments, anger, or fear in their facial expressions. I create questions based upon these various emotions I see. There is a light that is thrown over them, which tells me certain things."

"Let me take a guess," he interrupted. "Most of the light that is thrown over your client's face comes from the eyes. Do you agree?"

"Yes, I think so. I think it's the eyes more than anything they say to me. In fact, I have never offered to go very far with anyone unless I get this meaningful picture."

They had frequent discussions along these lines. Gabriella became convinced that she was relying rather heavily on some kind of signal coming from a person's eyes.

Aaron's memories flowed as though he were there with them. Their stories lived in him. He had heard them told and retold throughout his childhood, and always they conjured visions in his mind of those times and of the grandparents whose lives impacted so many others. He felt at times that he carried their memories and sensed a strong connection to his grandmother's talent for reading the eyes. Since he experienced the odd sensation trying to play the parlor trick for Sara, he now found himself skittish about the whole thing, but at the same time it kept returning to his mind.

Chapter 5

Aaron missed his family most of all at night. Being away from his parents offered him certain freedoms that he had never had, but at the same time he felt more than a twinge of longing for his father's forthright manner and his mother's caring gestures. As soon as he completed his studies and retired for the night, he found himself reliving the memories of childhood when his grandparents were always close at hand. He easily could have filled a book with their stories of life and their experience and wisdom.

Through the religious and social functions of the synagogue, Filip met a new, younger physician, Henry K. Walczak, a bone doctor who had spent a year in England working with Sir Robert Jones, an outstanding leader in the new specialty of orthopedic medicine which made extensive and successful use of the innovative concept of splinting broken and shattered bones.

Aaron recalled the happiness revealed on his grandfather's face as he spoke of those times. On one particular evening, Filip and Henry found themselves deep in conversation over a few glasses of wine. Their subject, rarely discussed in those days, was the business aspect of medical practice. They were both keenly aware of the fact that most of the revenue they drew in fees from patients was spent on overhead costs such as administrative salaries, laboratory space and equipment, nurses, and various medical assistants. As the time and bottles of wine passed that evening, they discovered that these overhead expenses could be shared by two doctors at much less than twice the cost for one physician. It became clear that a combination of both practices would help both the doctors and their patients, so they formed a joint practice in newly furnished and equipped offices in downtown Danzig. The local papers carried the news, and a special announcement was made in the synagogue.

The practice flourished. Reception rooms were always filled with waiting patients, and their reputations as the best in the area grew.

The two physicians were proud of building a medical practice which improved the health and longevity of their patients in the Danzig community and neighboring towns. The men worked hard to bring wealth and stability for their families. Their practice continually challenged their intellect and skills, but a deep, nagging feeling pervaded their lives. While the relationship between the Jews and the Danzig governmental offices appeared smooth and stable, Jewish history throughout Europe over the centuries taught them that time was not on their side.

While historians of the future would refer to this period as post-war/pre-war, that designation would have seemed quite absurd at the time. Equally unlikely, a day was coming in the not-too-distant future when these two doctors and their clinic would provide one of the most heartwarming stories of thousands of Jews who were rescued from destruction by their neighbors and countrymen under great personal risk.

In March 1920, the Seitners had their first child, a boy they named Jeremy. The delivery was an exhausting process for Gabriella, and she lay in bed for several days afterward to regain her strength. When she returned to her routine with the help of a nurse for the child, she felt moody and wept frequently. Filip recognized her situation as a kind of depression that often follows childbirth.

She met with her friend Janina, Henry's wife, for several days over lunch to discuss her state of mind.

"Filip thinks that I need a change of scenery," Gabriella said.

"Yes, I think we should go to Berlin and Munich to spend a couple of days shopping, spending our husbands' money," Janina suggested.

"I've heard about the earthshaking speeches by a new politician, Adolph Hitler, I believe is his name. He is extremely emotional, very angry about the rotten deal Germany was given in the treaty. I heard that his audience are suspended as if in a trance. I think I need to be shaken up like that. Yes, let's go to Munich for a few days."

They agreed to leave as soon as all arrangements could be made, and only a few days later the two friends found themselves in Germany. As the crowd gathered to hear the speeches of the Nazi leaders, Gabriella and Janina, arriving early, found themselves in a position to hear the speakers and see their facial expressions. Gabriella listened and absorbed Hitler's words. At times he seemed to be gazing directly at her. She could see deeply into his eyes.

After the crowd disbanded, they entered a nearby coffee shop. Janina shook her head in disbelief. "My father has talked endlessly about how the Treaty of Versailles was dangerously unfair to the German people who have been weakened economically and militarily with little hope of gaining any status in the near future."

Gabriella asked, "Why do you say *dangerously*?"

"Because Hitler is blaming the Jews. He's making us scapegoats as if somehow Jews had written the terms of the treaty and put the German nation in the weak position that they find themselves."

As Gabriella listened to her friend, she tried to organize the array of feelings the speech encompassed. Yes, there was irrational blaming. *What benefit does he derive through such propaganda?* And yet she had sensed a dangerous element to the speech. She felt a premonition that somehow Hitler would seek revenge against Jews in spite of the fact that he was a new and unsupported politician with crazy ideas.

"Do you believe, Janina, that Hitler can cause harm to the Jewish people? I feel that he can, and it scares me that I don't know how he can harm us."

"No," Janina replied. "I think he's just a lot of hot air who's trying to arouse hatred.

* * *

During Gabriella's absence, Filip spent more than the usual amount of time discussing current events with Henry. It was a subject that interested them greatly and helped pass the time during some of the more routine aspects of their work.

When their wives returned, Filip was particularly interested in hearing Gabriella's impressions of Hitler.

"I thought by now you would have had a lot to say about your trip and particularly the speeches you heard," Filip said. "In fact, you seem quite pensive since your return."

"Pensive may not be the exact word for my mood," she responded. "I am quite under a spell from listening to and watching that man."

"Well, in general, did you find him to be a noisy, emotional politician seeking support, or, at the other extreme, was he an upcoming politician who could be dangerous if granted support from the people?"

"To be honest I am frightened by that man," his wife said quietly. "I thought by now I would have released such strong feelings, but they stay with me, and I don't exactly understand why they continue to do this to me."

She went silent for several moments, looking off into the distance. Finally, she turned toward her husband and spoke intently.

"There were times during the speeches when he seemed to be looking directly at me, and there was a strange look, a presence, in his eyes. I saw a tremendous amount of pent-up anger. Yes, I've heard and read a lot about how Jews are not welcome and were not wanted in any of the businesses. We all know how we are hated. You would think I would be used to that kind of thing by now; however, right now I feel like I would like to run and hide."

Listening to her, Filip felt tension taking over his body and a pronounced pounding of his heart as he realized the commonality between Gabriella's impressions and reactions and some of what he heard recently from Henry.

* * *

Aaron shuddered as he recalled his grandparents' stories about that time. In hindsight, his grandmother's impressions about Hitler certainly proved true—to the devastation of countless lives and the loss of more than a million Jewish souls. If only others had discerned in the man's eyes the evil that Aaron's grandmother had seen.

Chapter 6

In subsequent years, Filip and Gabriella's prominence in the community grew. Their young son became strong and self-confident. Gabriella kept busy as a homemaker and friend to her neighbors.

All the while, her memories of Hitler remained clear and unaltered. She asked herself many times why he frightened her so. In her conversations with Filip, she often referred to the darkness she saw in his face.

"I never saw such darkness on anybody's face," she repeated often. "You know we often refer to troublesome events or circumstances as 'the darkest days' or we say someone is 'in a dark mood.'"

"Yes, I know," Filip replied.

"All I can tell is that, despite the sunny day, all I could detect when I watched him was darkness," Gabriella said solemnly.

"Many say he's just a troublemaker with a lot of noise," Filip said. "But the fact is his party is growing and getting more and more seats in parliament. Most people believe he is not well liked or respected and that his days of power will always be limited."

In reality, Hitler's speeches became louder, more forceful, as his emotions intensified. At the core of his hatred was the as yet unproved accusations that Versailles was about blaming Germany for the war and blaming the Jews for attempting in turn to set the world against Germany.

* * *

Nineteen-thirty was a turning point in European history. Hitler's Nazi party grew to 18 percent of the German Parliament, and it appeared that he was on his way to becoming Chancellor of Germany.

As Gabriella read about Hitler's rise to power, her thoughts returned to her experience in Munich. Again, she tried to describe the confusing images that she saw while listening to this rising dictator.

"There was such darkness in his face, in his eyes. Some shadowy design that confused me. Even now, I think of the icy darkness obscuring that sunny day."

"Darkness, I'm sure you know, represents so many ideas in our culture," her husband said. "When we think of angels, for example, we think of light emanating. Our image of peace and tranquility is usually bright and sunny. Darkness, on the other hand, is usually associated with bad things, with fear, evil, hopelessness. You saw and listened to this man blame the Jews for all of Germany's troubles in such an emotional presentation where he seemed to be tearing his guts out in anger. Whatever you perceived about him would have been delivered to you in a very dark picture. At the same time, you have me thinking that these impressions you frequently get through others' eyes are an amazing gift or skill. One could take what you saw at that time as a warning."

"Yes, I think you're right. Seeing him, it was like I was confronted with the devil himself, and I saw only bad times and destruction—things that only evil people or forces can bring to us. I sensed another world war."

* * *

Aaron's recollection of his family's retelling of those events often left him feeling shaken. He was grateful those days were in the past. But he knew that the gift his grandmother carried, the ability to see the truth in someone's eyes, was passed down to him. He hoped he could use it to affect something positive in his work as an attorney someday. But for now, his consciousness nagged at him as he remembered the strange shadow lurking in the eyes of someone who, on the surface, seemed charming and kind.

Chapter 7

Despite a glimpse of something troubling as he gazed into Sara's eyes, Aaron continued to spend time with her. She was an excellent study partner and a beautiful woman. He hadn't noticed the odd feeling about her eyes again, but the thought of what he sensed as he peered into them continued to nag at him from time to time.

Nonetheless, Aaron hoped for more from the relationship than having a study partner. The enticing elements of their first meetings held such promise, and although he sensed she was by nature flirtatious, he also felt she was attracted to him despite the fact that they hadn't kissed again since their second encounter. They had gone on four dates, but she always met him at the restaurant or movie theater and then left him swiftly at the end of each evening after he saw her home.

One afternoon as they sat on their favorite bench on a particularly warm September day, he thought it was time to say something.

"Sara, I think I must have gotten the wrong impression about you when we met. Are you only interested in me as a friend?"

"I do consider you a friend, Aaron, but I also feel something more than that. Why else would I keep going out with you?"

"Well, you haven't given me so much as a peck on the cheek since that time we kissed before we went out."

Sara sat quietly for a few moments, appearing to gather her thoughts. Finally, she turned and looked at him.

"When you and I kissed, we were here on campus. Standing outside my parents' doorway, I just felt...Well, I couldn't be sure my father wasn't watching," she said. "As I've gotten older, he's become stricter and stricter. As long as I live at home and he pays for my education, I'm bound by his rules. When I consented to go into law, which wasn't what I had hoped for my life, I agreed to stay at home to save the cost of campus housing. Now, here I am at 24, and I feel trapped in a house where I'm treated like a petulant child or a wayward teenager."

Aaron inched closer to her on the bench and put an arm around her shoulder. "I'm sorry," he said. "I didn't realize your father was so strict."

Sara leaned against his shoulder for a moment and then sat straight again, looking into his eyes. "It wasn't always this way. He's been especially odd lately. It's like all he cares about are appearances, showing the world that he, his wife, and his only child are upstanding members of the community. I feel like he watches me all the time, and he seems overly concerned about what I'm doing outside of law school. A couple of times...I don't know for sure, but I would swear he has followed me. I can't imagine why he would. I must be wrong about that.

"But he's definitely been acting strangely. Once, not long ago, he said that I reminded him too much of himself. But I don't get that at all. I'm much more like my mother in every way that matters. And the truth is I'm my own person, or at least I'm trying to be if my parents would let me.

"You should have seen his face when he told me I was too much like him. The look in his eyes was so peculiar. I felt as if he were saying it was a curse to be like him. And, just in that moment, I really hoped he was wrong because I felt like some dark cloud was hanging over him. I don't know. I suppose I was just imagining things."

Aaron couldn't help wondering if her words related to what he had seen in her eyes while playing his parlor game on their first date, but he said nothing. He just embraced her a little more tightly and considered ways he could make her life more tolerable.

"I'm sorry to burden you with any of this," she said. "I mean, the truth is I have a good life. I have a great education, all the comforts and nice things I could desire. I just feel sometimes that I'm not living my own life."

"I suppose we all feel that way sometimes," Aaron replied. "Our parents, our grandparents, our culture, everyone has their expectations of how we should behave and what we should become. I get how that can weigh on a person. Sometimes our lives are shaped by those expectations. Your direction just seems more obviously influenced than mine, but I suspect most of us find ourselves walking a path that isn't entirely of our own making."

"I think you may be wise beyond your years," she said. One of her enigmatic grins greeted him when she lifted her face toward his. She pressed her palm gently but firmly against his cheek and kissed him. When she pulled back, she smiled again and said, "Now, you can't say I haven't kissed you since we first met."

Aaron saw no trace of shadow in her eyes as the sunlight danced in them and her playful quality returned.

The two of them had research to do that afternoon for their term papers, so they strolled together across campus to the library. They trudged up the marble steps of the massive gray-white building, carrying satchels laden with law books and notepaper. As they entered, the scent of old books overtook their senses. High arched walls made of aged stone drew the eyes upward to ornately carved ceiling panels. Aaron always found himself in awe when entering here.

"This library reminds me of how I'd rather be spending my days," Sara whispered. "Drenched in an ocean of books. Give me a card catalog and stacks upon stacks of books, and I'm one happy girl."

Aaron noticed Sara's entire demeanor seemed to shift when they entered the library. He hadn't realized until just that instant that her shoulders had been lifted and tight before they came into this space. Now, her posture relaxed, and she seemed to feel at home. She would have made the prettiest librarian he had ever seen if she could have gone down that road instead of veering onto the path of law.

It was time to go their separate ways up into the stacks to find the volumes each would need for their chosen topics. Sara spent a few minutes with one of the library assistants to get her advice on where to go while Aaron, who had already started his research, was ready to navigate the stairs and locate the section of books he needed. He lost track of Sara in the process and simply dug into the work. He found a quiet nook with a study corner nearby and pulled two references.

As he opened the first volume, he felt a strange sensation as if he were being watched. He heard a sound nearby and caught the merest glimpse of a man in a dark grey fedora, who quickly darted into the stacks. When Aaron went to find him, the only things present were rows of shelves and countless books.

Chapter 8

For a while in his early years, Aaron had considered following in his grandfather's footsteps and becoming a doctor. He was so proud of his grandparents' gifts and considered their legacy an important part of his life.

The availability of aspirin coincided with his grandfather's medical school years and early clinical work. Extracts of willow tree bark were used for centuries in the treatment of fever, pain, and inflammation. In the mid-19th century, chemists isolated and identified the active compound salicylic acid, and this led to the manufacture and distribution of its powder form. While the use of this medicine by the end of the century had grown considerably, the unpleasant side effects, including gastric irritation, limited its helpfulness. The discovery of the acetyl derivative of salicylic acid known as aspirin, introduced in the early 20th century, substantially reduced irritation. And notably the new drug in tablet form was provided to doctors in the United States and Europe, requesting their written evaluations which would be compiled and distributed for general use.

Filip Seitner was particularly interested in the observation that aspirin could substantially reduce fever associated with childhood diseases and became involved in the life-saving applications and benefits of using aspirin in pediatric practice. His name appeared on the summary of reports by doctors all over the world who were claiming the multiple benefits of aspirin in treating pain and reducing fever.

In his medical practice, Filip maintained an intense interest in the new drug aspirin and carefully followed the results he obtained with his patients and particularly with children having childhood diseases. He kept careful records which he shared with the manufacturer in Germany who in return compiled results from all the doctors in Europe in a bulletin sent out to all hospitals and clinics.

In reviewing the published results of aspirin therapy, Filip was particularly interested in those by Swedish Physician Dr. Theo Svensson, who was similarly active in treating the dangerous fevers associated with childhood diseases. Based on this common interest, he decided to write Svensson to share their medical interests in more detail. Eventually the exchange of letters became more detailed, more comprehensive, and more personal. They shared a great admiration for each other's success in rescuing sick children.

Later in his letters to Svensson, Filip introduced some political thoughts. He mentioned the growing strength of Hitler's Nazi Party and wondered if the Nazis were gaining support in Sweden. He also spoke of his concerns over the unlawful military buildup in Germany.

In response, Svensson wrote that the Nazi Socialist Party had not gained any significant backing in Sweden, probably because there were established socialist parties in existence which continued to maintain the support of most of the Swedish population. He volunteered that in Sweden Hitler was considered aggressive in a threatening way, someone who could disturb the balance in Europe and possibly start a war. People talked with each other about these issues only to confirm that, in case of such a war, Sweden would remain neutral and would enjoy a continuing trade with Germany for agricultural products.

Svensson was happy to report that the recently created Ministry of Health and Social Affairs formed by the socialist government of Sweden under Dr. Niels Bireland maintained a political platform which promised high standards of health care for the entire population. It was no secret that in order to reach this goal Sweden needed many more professional medical practitioners, more clinics, and better education of the people regarding health and safety in their lives.

When Theo Svensson first started to picture the Polish doctor with whom he had been exchanging letters, he thought it would be outrageous and certainly asking too much for him to give up his practice and his clinic and bring his wife and children to a completely new culture and geography. But he could not get it out of his mind, and after a while his thoughts started to rationalize such a move. After all, the ministry with its new commitment to medical growth would certainly support Filip with facilities funds and anything else he needed to build a practice in Sweden. He envisioned the Seitners as new friends. His wife would be more than willing to introduce them to the people he knew who would make the Seitners feel at home. Finally, in a subsequent letter, he wrote:

> *My dear colleague Dr. Seitner,*
>
> *While I hesitate to make the suggestion since it is such a major change for you and your family, I do rationalize that you and your family could count on a secure life, free from political threats here in Sweden with professional medical support from the government, which would be most anxious to add*

you to the fine albeit tiny staff of physicians in Stockholm. Would you kindly consider a meeting to discuss this idea in more detail? Also, there is so much in medicine that we could discuss face to face. Perhaps we could select London as a midpoint for such a meeting.

Yours truly,
Your friend and colleague,
Theo Svensson, M.D.

The letter from Dr. Svensson was one of the mementos of the past Aaron's grandparents had saved through the years. It changed their lives and may have saved them from a terrible fate, so they shared the story with their grandson many times.

Chapter 9

Aaron had been told countless stories about his grandparents and his father's life as a boy and young man. Learning about his family history was integrated into his education about Jewish history, and much of Aaron's life was steeped in both. In his own childhood, he loved to hear about what life was like for his father and grandparents.

With the help of housekeepers who assisted her with the everyday chores, Gabriella Seitner, Aaron's grandmother, spent many happy hours teaching Swedish customs and language to his father Jeremy. As a child, Jeremy took a keen interest in his religious studies and was particularly fascinated by the history of the Jewish people.

Growing up both in Poland and Sweden in an environment where anti-Semitism was well entrenched, Jeremy learned to accept it as part of his life. Most parents felt their children would face the realities and this form of hatred soon enough. On several occasions, the Hebrew school classes had the privilege of listening to leaders of the Zionists movement. Jeremy was fascinated by the concept of building a new nation free of anti-Semitism.

While recognizing that the lines were not always clear and distinct, Jews who inhabited Eastern Europe in the early 20th century identified themselves as belonging to one of three main groups. First there were the observant Jews, who followed the teachings of the Torah under the guidance of a scholarly rabbi. Preserving strict Jewish teachings was never considered an easy path; nevertheless, observant Jews felt rewarded as they adhered to the teachings their maker expected of them. Most countries placed severe restrictions on Jews pertaining to the lands and the professions available. Observant Jews followed their religious practices under harsh conditions but found happiness through teaching their children to practice the Sabbath and Jewish holidays together.

Among European Jews, a second division could be found. A trace of secularism was spreading in Europe as well as in the United States. Those who embraced this philosophy were less adherent to Jewish law but were socially and professionally identified with the most modern and well-educated in the country.

The third and growing group of Jews maintained an intense awareness of the fact that Jerusalem was mentioned so many times in Jewish prayer and literature that they could hardly forget the ties that bound them to the Holy Land. These people prayed for the day when they might return. Realizing that the Holy Land was not nearly as advanced technologically as Europe, they dedicated themselves and their lives to bringing that homeland into the modern age. But first they had to learn how to farm using rudimentary and basic equipment in order to sustain themselves as they tried to create these small, up-to-date communities.

Zionist groups formed throughout Europe as Jews increasingly dreamt of a homeland, a nation for and by Jews. Zionism was most active in Poland. With his growing interest, Jeremy was pleased to learn this.

Chapter 10

One of the traditions Aaron loved most from his upbringing was the frequent sharing of family history. Oral accounts were an important means of instilling values, engaging children in their heritage, and keeping their culture alive through hardships and difficult times. One of Aaron's favorite pastimes throughout his childhood was hearing about what his father's life had been like growing up in Europe. A favorite story had always been how he met Aaron's mother and how their lives began. He had even begun a journal as a child to keep the stories alive and continued to refer to it as a resource for recalling what was important.

After graduating from high school, his father Jeremy had traveled to Kraków, the second largest city in Poland. Containing half of the Jewish population in the country, Kraków was becoming a major center of Jewish life, culture, and learning. Jeremy wanted to live and learn among Europe's most avid Zionists, and this is what he pictured for himself in the next year or two. After that, well, he would wait and see. He needed a job to make some money. How he would find time to do so much seemed a little tricky, but he would figure that out.

He was fortunate in scheduling a private meeting with Osias Thorn who had brought Zionist ideology to the city and who became the undisputed leader of the Kraków Jews.

"So you are the son of Dr. Filip Seitner?" he said as they sat down. "His work is well-known here. Such *Mitzvot!!*"

"Yes, sir," Jeremy replied. He quickly observed the bare walls and basic furniture of the Zionist leader's office. "I would like to begin Zionist training and participate in the growing cultural and intellectual life here," he said fervently.

"You are welcome here. Let me offer some help in getting started. First, I shall find a family for you to get your room and board. You will no doubt share modest daily expenses with them. I will also get you into a work-study group, which will help in getting your ideas straight about going to Palestine permanently. Our culture has been changing quite rapidly during the last 50 to 100 years. Of course, always with some disagreement among our people. A major controversy has revolved around language, but that seems to have been resolved at least partially. We no longer talk in old fashioned Yiddish. Now it's in Hebrew and Polish. We believe that using the Polish language is a sure sign of our dedication to the country in which we reside.

"Let me share just a little history. After centuries of persecution and expulsion, Jews of the diaspora found comfort in dreaming of a return to the Holy Land. This idea, which you can find in literature and emotionally powerful songs and prayers over many decades, was a constant reminder of a new hope in the future. Driven by relentless expulsion and intolerance, the dream became a reality in the late 18th century. Jewish emigration started mainly with small farming groups. Under continued religious persecution, Jews in increasing numbers chose the option of returning to Palestine, and as a result supportive Zionist groups formed over Europe with a notable concentration in Eastern Europe. Zionist camps formed around the Kraków area where students came to learn about and experience their heritage. We are participants in Kraków life, but at the same time we live and work in groups which emphasize farming, plumbing, and carpentry, and the Hebrew language as practiced today in Palestine. These groups function as a steppingstone for those who decide to make Palestine their future home."

Jeremy listened attentively to every word Osias Thorn spoke. He noticed the man's eyes held a kind of yearning as he spoke of Palestine.

"I suppose you would like to find a job," the leader continued. "I can't help you on that search. You'll just have to go door to door and introduce yourself. Stand up tall. You're about six feet tall, right? Dress well and speak slowly and firmly."

* * *

There was peace in Poland and a reasonably fair economy. The Jewish people had as good a welcome there as they had ever had. The Polish railway system was growing rapidly with increased demands for new stations and tracks. People were traveling more, exploring the country, visiting friends and relatives, and enjoying the wonderful new spas that were opening around the nation. As a result, railroad personnel were strained at running the system effectively. One emerging problem related to the increasing number of checked baggage. Because the cars were full, suitcases were piled up in the little space available. No good procedures for handling checked bags existed. Frequently travelers lost track of their luggage, which ended up in the train station unclaimed.

Jeremy introduced himself as a prospective employee who was strong in both body and intelligence. At six feet tall with large shoulders and arms, he made a favorable first impression. His facial features were prominent yet friendly.

Deep in thought, the chief officer of the Kraków railroad station stared at Jeremy a moment. He had no openings; yet he saw this young man as both physically and intellectually capable. He had a sense that Jeremy was a problem solver who could get things done and decided to hire him.

As a new employee of the Polish railway system, Jeremy took on the task of learning all the stations and timetables. He studied both at work and at home until he knew the system. He was given the assignment of figuring out how to manage increasing numbers of lost bags. This problem offered the kind of challenge he liked, and he spent his spare time searching for a solution.

After convincing the station master to give him the service of a company carpenter, he began constructing strong boxes about five feet high and six feet deep with doors that swung open wide enough to take a suitcase. He proposed building about 20 of these boxes to be placed in rows adjacent to the south end of the station, where there was sufficient unused space. Each box was marked for identification. He recommended that suitcases left unattended be recorded by name and address and held in the stored box location. All suitcases would be protected from thieves and from foul weather and could be easily retrieved with the owner's name. His new system was enacted and seemed to improve the situation.

* * *

In addition to his job at the railroad station, Jeremy spent long days learning to farm. When he returned home after a full day in the field, he felt aches and pains in his back and legs beyond any he had ever experienced. The heat from hours beneath the sun lingered, and he could not seem to quench his thirst.

He noticed that the women in his crew worked just as hard and were as dedicated as the men. Their conversation was limited to Zionist principles. They were there to learn farming as they would find it in Palestine. They wore no makeup or perfume, and the poorer ones worked only in a bra and worn-out shorts. Back in the kitchen after laboring in the fields, there was no socializing; they were there to get some food together for themselves.

Most of the women were not particularly attractive, but one caught his interest. She was tall and slightly muscular with light brunette hair tied back. He found himself staring at her lovely face. She appeared lively, happy, and intelligent.

A little later Jeremy became aware that she was gazing at him. He looked over to her, and she gave him a smile he would never forget. They glanced at each other often as both wore a warm, friendly smile. They hadn't said a word to each other, yet it felt as though they'd known each other for a long time.

On subsequent workdays walking back from the field, he strolled alongside her with his arm around her waist, and she reciprocated. One evening cool breezes beckoned him outside into the gardens, where he met her alone. They still had said little to each other.

"What is your name, dear man?" she asked.

"My name is Jeremy, and who are you?"

"I am Anna."

An unspoken understanding passed between them. Words were unnecessary.

He reached out for her and kissed her. She put her hands on his face. The perfume from her shower soap had worn off, and he could only detect the enchanting oils from her body.

He thought of Anna frequently as he tried to fall asleep that night. he had never experienced such closeness to a woman. They seemed so comfortable with each other as if they had known each other for a long time. *Is this what it feels like to have a soulmate*, he wondered.

After a week of work at the railroad and another long day in the fields at the Zionist camp, he lay down on a small cot in a large dormitory. He found himself unable to sleep despite his exhaustion. Rising to explore his surroundings in the dimness of the dormitory, Jeremy softly paced the room scanning the occupants of the various cots until finally he found hers. Unspoken words floated in the air between them, and he held her close, her heart beating against his. *We belong to each other. And together we will fulfill the Zionist dreams of the last century.* After a kiss goodnight, he returned to his own cot and welcomed sleep.

After a couple of months of these shared moments, they married in a simple ceremony with a rabbi from one of the nearby synagogues. Their parents could not attend because they were given little notice to travel such a distance. Only their associates were there to wish them well.

Jeremy and his new wife spent time crystallizing their plans to help build a new homeland for the Jews. He would leave behind his family and his good job with the railroad and what appeared to be the prospect of many years of peace and prosperity with Jews and Christians living side-by-side. Even then, they encountered some anti-Semitism but nothing serious.

They became increasingly dedicated to the idea of a new homeland in Palestine and began planning a move in the next year or two. During that span they would improve their farming skills and learn to speak everyday Hebrew.

This was a peak period for Jewish life in Poland. Many joined in with the Polish people in a spirit of nationalism. While Jews were at that time asked to leave most European countries, the Polish government extended them a secure life integrated with the Polish people and hopefully with a minimum of anti-Semitism. So the couple enjoyed the cultural and social initiatives of the city while training for future life in Palestine.

Probably no time in Jewish history held such hopes for a bright and happy future. But those dreams were dashed quickly and with finality when the Nazis invaded and occupied Poland in 1939 and began ordering the expulsion of all Jews out of their homes and into prison camps. In the following weeks, the Jews of Kraków and the adjoining farms, towns, and villages were given dates and times to appear at the railroad station. People were stunned. Their futures suddenly darkened as if a window shade was pulled down completely blocking the sun.

At the last possible moment, Jeremy and Anna gathered their possessions and took a bus to the Kraków train station, arriving on the platform at the time and place that they were assigned. Jeremy reminded her to be aware of his movements. He told her to watch his body for any motion, any sign he might make to direct her. They prearranged signals that would mean to move slowly or quickly in a certain direction; she acknowledged. They tended to stay to rear of the gathering crowd at the train station platform. The group grew to least two hundred with more coming. The guards stood beyond the crowd but edged closer as the train stopped. Jeremy again nudged her towards the back of the crowd and the south edge of the train station. Amid the throng of people, the two of them moved back as the doors opened. There was a commotion and delays in getting into the cars. The guards became distracted and were forced to come closer to the trouble spots where bottlenecks of people stumbled, crying and begging to be excused. Jeremy directed his and Anna's movements in such a way that placed them only yards away from his large suitcase lockers at side of the station. He kept watching for uproar among the crowds and the distraction of the guards in front of the open doors of the train. He finally gave her a hard push towards the lockers. He ran and she followed. He reached the rear of the second row. Kneeling down and opening one of the boxes with his key, he helped her through the opening and then got in himself. After closing the door behind them, he pushed some of suitcases towards the front so that they could stretch out and hide behind them.

"We'll be safe here," he whispered to her. "No one knows about these lockers except me and a few of my associates."

Anna stared ahead, her face expressionless.

"There will be a freight train to Warsaw around midnight for us to hop on," he said. "And then we can make connections to the coast and a ferry boat from Gdansk to Stockholm and my parent's home."

Chapter 11

It was midafternoon when they arrived at the Gdansk ferry landings. The ticket counter stood on the pier about 30 yards from the boat. People were lined up to purchase tickets and some already stood facing the ticket taker on the stern of the boat. Four young German guards, not taking their duties very seriously, were keeping their eyes on their wristwatches as they talked about what a long day it had been and how much they wanted their dinner. Of the four men, one was noticeably shorter and thinner with a serious look on his face. He seemed to enjoy the fact that he had been given authority to capture and maybe even shoot escaping Jews. This young man had never excelled in physical activities at school and was mediocre at practically everything he had ever tried. This new opportunity was perhaps tailormade for his weakened ego. Unlike the other three, he scanned the area vigilantly for any suspicious activity.

Jeremy and Anna stood out of sight in the shadows of a nearby building. They carefully watched the crowd movements, the boat, and the guards. As the 5 o'clock scheduled embarking time approached, the workers began to clear the chain and rope attachments between boat and pier. The last of the passengers moved from the stern of the boat to the stairs leading up to the passengers' quarters. The guards turned their backs to the boat and began to slowly walk away, focusing their attention in a new direction. Only the smaller of the four nervously glanced around the area for anything irregular.

The sound of the engine at low idle could be heard as late afternoon shadows began to cover the dock. Jeremy and Anna quickly approached the boat as it was slowly pulling away from the pier. They jumped about five feet to land on the stern. Jeremy ran slightly ahead and soon reached the top of the stairs and the upper platform leading to the passengers' area. She was a little slower and kept turning around as she climbed the steps. Noticing this movement, the smaller guard left his friends and started running toward the boat. He jumped and reached the staircase as the vessel began to make its sharp westerly turn toward Sweden. Anna looked down from the top the stairs and froze as she saw him at the bottom of the steps. The boat gradually picked up speed maintaining its sharp left turn.

The guard held his rifle in both hands and pointed it at Anna, but the force of the turn caused him to be thrown against the railing, which he leaned against in order to stabilize himself as he grasped the rifle in both hands. Jeremy returned to the top the stairs and looked down at the pursuing guard, who maintained a precarious position. Without a thought, he quickly lowered his head and flew down the stairs, his large shoulders hitting the German in the midsection. He could hear air escaping from the small man's lungs and could feel the rifle between their bodies. Using all his strength he pushed up against the smaller man, elevating him over the railing and then into a downward fall. Hitting headfirst on the edge of the boat, the German guard fell lifeless into the wake of the boat.

Anna ran into his arms. He guided her into the passenger quarters, where she sat beside him trembling and sobbing. They sipped wine as he tried to reassure her.

"If you count to 200, we'll be about halfway to Sweden," he said. Far from being accurate, such a silly statement gave them something to laugh at.

Jeremy began thinking about his future in Sweden. With Europe dominated by the German Army and Jews throughout Europe being rounded up for extermination, their Zionist plans were put on a back burner. They had a lot of thinking to do.

They arrived at the clinic by taxi about 3:30 in the morning. The night watchman opened the heavy front door and used a flashlight to identify them.

"Is that you, Jeremy?" he said. "The doctor has been so worried about you. Please sit down. I will go get him and your mother; she has been terribly worried."

After Jeremy and Anna showered, they joined his parents for an enormous breakfast. He described the Zionist camps and the high spirits of the people in Kraków. Then he related how they narrowly escaped Poland.

"Everyone was so shocked at how quickly the Germans started to round up people for concentration camps. We barely got out in time. It was close. And we were scared…"

His wife spoke up. "You should have seen him," she told his parents. "Jeremy was so brave and so strong. I simply held on and followed him. I will never forget how confident he was. A true hero!"

After many questions and catching up with each other, they paused the conversation. His parents needed to absorb everything they had heard.

His mother Gabriella broke the silence.

"Jeremy, let me look at your face carefully," she said. She studied his eyes slowly with a partial smile, and then, as the smile disappeared, she put her head on the table and cried softly.

"What do you see?" Jeremy asked. He put his hand gently on her shoulder.

She raised her head proudly exclaiming, "I see an image of a beautiful flag blowing in the wind, a beautiful white and blue flag with a large star of David."

* * *

As he grew up, Aaron had heard the stories of his parents and his grandparents as they dealt with the Nazi invasion of Europe and their goals to take over the world. The day that his parents successfully escaped from the German occupation in Poland always was prominent in his mind. In particular, he wondered whether his parents had experienced fear during the narrow escape that could have cost them their lives. The time finally came when he had felt comfortable asking his father about that harrowing experience.

As a boy he had said to his father, "I tried to imagine how frightened I would've been considering the fact that it would have been an immediate bullet had you been caught."

"To answer your question, I must tell you a few things about what I knew about your mother back then. During some of our earliest conversations, I remember how my mind drifted away from what she was saying as my focus was pulled into what I saw deep within her. Your mother had a longing to help people, to save lives. When I looked into her eyes, I saw that clearly, and I knew that this deep desire of hers would be fulfilled. I felt it with every fiber of my being. Therefore, I felt no fear of arrest or any other event that would prevent this wish of hers from becoming fulfilled. After I perceived such clear emotion and intention in her, it was as if that future was already written. I came to believe that nothing would stop us."

Aaron's admiration for his parents and their courage grew each time he listened to the tale of their escape. His father's determination to ensure that his mother's dreams came true made him feel proud, and he hoped to someday become as great a man as his father and grandfather.

Chapter 12

Aaron's parents were hardly the only ones to find courage in the midst of the Nazi invasions. On the morning of April 9, 1940, the people of Copenhagen were shocked upon finding their streets crowded with German troops and their sky full of German airplanes. Denmark had been neutral in WWI and was the only Scandinavian country to sign a nonaggression pact with the Nazis in the post-war period. As the world watched Germany overcome Western Europe, it understood why Denmark had done nothing by way of protection against a German invasion.

That same morning the German government offered the following notice to the Danes:

"In accordance with the great spirit which has always prevailed in Dutch-German relations, the German government declares that Germany does not intend now or in the future to interfere with Denmark's territorial integrity or political independence."

The Jewish community of Denmark, about 8000 people living in Copenhagen or the neighboring vicinity, were essentially left alone to live in peace. Some speculated that the reason for this change in German policy was that there was a spirit of common heritage between many Danes and Germans. The German Army was dependent on Denmark for agricultural products including dairy and grains; it would not be wise to disturb the delicate peace.

By mid-1943, events of the war were turning against the Nazis, so Hitler took steps to increase his broad control. On September 29, 1943, the news leaked to Jewish leaders that the Germans were planning to arrest all Danish Jews within the coming days, including during the Jewish High Holidays, for shipment to concentration camps.

It fell upon the rabbi of the Copenhagen synagogue to make an announcement to his congregation that the situation was grave. They must contact all of their relatives and friends to spread the word. He gave them two or three hours to leave their homes and go into hiding on the coast to be ferried over to safety in Sweden.

The Danes were asked to volunteer trucks, buses, and ambulances to rendezvous at Jewish homes, bringing thousands to the coast where they would hide until loaded onto small boats for Sweden. Danish civil leaders worked around the clock tirelessly to identify the Jewish families and their locations. Torn pages from phone books with names encircled were passed between them. Hundreds of fishing boats were enlisted to make the one-hour trip across the Oresund to Sweden. For those who could not afford to compensate the fishermen, Copenhagen citizens raised a small fortune to help pay their way.

Everyone worked quietly and efficiently, knowing the German officials were just a couple of hours behind them and ready to arrest anyone for participating in this rescue. Miraculously over 90% of the Jewish population was successfully rescued. At the end of the war when the Danes were asked about their immense courage, they simply shrugged it off as "the right thing to do."

The Swedish government offered assistance to the refugees in getting them settled. Doctors in particular, including the Svensson-Seitner Clinic in Stockholm, were asked to make contact as soon as possible. The refugees who had relatives in the Helsingborg area found temporary living quickly. For others, the trip to Stockholm was a full day by car. Within a period of weeks, all of the refugees found permanent apartments and eventually jobs.

Soon after the refugees landed, Filip Seitner made the long trip to Helsingborg, found available space, and began seeing patients overcome by fear immediately. In sympathy with their Danish neighbors, local citizens joined him in offering emergency food and clothing and living space. Among the well-meaning Swedes offering his services to Filip was the seemingly caring and sympathetic Edvin Karlsson.

Chapter 13

Aaron and Sara continued to see each other both for study sessions and outside of law school as their budding relationship grew closer. The more she spoke of her father, the more he felt there might be something off about the man.

One day, a chance meeting guided him to understand the reason for his concerns. He was shopping downtown when he encountered Sara on an unusual outing with her parents. He entered the local drugstore to pick up a few toiletries and other items he couldn't find on campus. He spotted Sara in a polka dotted dress on one of the aisles. Her hair was pulled back away from her face, making her look younger, more like a teenager.

Intently scanning a shelf, she appeared lost in her search for some item. She hadn't noticed him walking toward her and seemed startled when he spoke her name.

"Aaron," she said, "what are you doing here?"

"Just out to pick up a few things."

Her usual charming, outgoing demeanor seemed absent as they conversed as though she were on edge for some reason. Aaron stood with his back toward the rear of the store as they spoke, and she faced him. He watched her smile wither and her eyes widen as she looked past him.

"We have what we need. It's time to go," a man's voice said from behind him.

"I'll just grab this off the shelf then," she said, quickly pulling down a manicure set.

Aaron turned to see the man who walked past him, his lovely blonde wife following a pace behind.

As the two reached Sara, she said, "Father, Mother, this is my friend Aaron, my study partner at law school. Mom, you remember me mentioning him."

Aaron reached out first to Mrs. Knight and then to Sara's father, who wore an expensive-looking suit and a fedora that was angled down slightly across his left eye. Aaron's gaze met his for only an instant but long enough to shake him. Aaron showed nothing on the outside and actually managed a strong, firm handshake and a steady appearance.

"We have to be leaving, Sara," Garland Knight said. "Take that up front to the register, and I'll pay for it."

Her father's eyes darted quickly toward the front of the store. He added, "Nice to meet you, young man," and then swiftly turned and walked away.

Sara waved goodbye as her parents ushered her toward the cash register. Aaron watched them check out and leave the store before he released a long sigh. It was only then that he realized he had been holding his breath since the handshake. He allowed a shudder to pass up his spine. He recognized what he had seen in those eyes. Although Aaron was almost always able to sense deceit and had a strong feeling about whether those he met were honest and honorable or the reverse, he seldom had encountered true evil. But he was overwhelmed with the knowing that there was something cold, dark, and sinister behind those eyes.

* * *

It was two weeks before the high holidays, and Aaron looked forward to going home to spend the occasion with his parents and to see his grandparents, who were coming to visit for Rosh Hashanah, which fell in October that year. His plans were made for the trip, but he still had to complete a fall-term writing project that was due in three weeks and keep up with his studies in preparation for midterms later in the month. His nose was buried in a book much of the time, and he had study dates with Sara four times a week. There was no shortage of things to occupy his thoughts. Nonetheless, he found himself more than once lying awake at night with those eyes, that gaze, staring back at him from beneath the brim of a charcoal grey fedora. He rubbed his eyes and tried to wipe away the memory, but still it lingered in his consciousness.

One day on a study date, Aaron decided to broach the subject with Sara. The man was her father, so he had to tread carefully.

"Sara, are you always timid around your father? When we met in the drugstore, I noticed—and maybe I'm wrong—but you seemed a little nervous around him. Of course, it was such a quick meeting that I couldn't really say for sure."

Aaron detected a slight shift of her features and body language. Her right shoulder drew back, and her face went blank for a moment before her usual pleasant smile returned.

"What's there to say about parents, right?" she said. "I guess you could say he's been even more… *stern* than usual lately. I suppose it's different for my parents, coming here from Sweden. I'm sure you understand since yours immigrated too, but it's not just that. You remember what I told you last week? I'm not sure my father even trusts me—or my mother for that matter. He just always seems to be looking over his shoulder. It's a strange thing to say, but I think once or twice he might have followed me to make sure I was going to campus. I know that sounds crazy."

Aaron recalled the odd feeling he had in the library and his glimpse of the man in a fedora who disappeared into the stacks. But he was wise enough to say nothing in response. He wondered what Garland Knight had to hide. Aaron's father once told him, "Only the untrustworthy trust no one," and he had found this to be true. Aaron decided to let the subject drop for now. He had no desire to stir up suspicion and ill feelings between Sara and her parents. He only wished he could protect her somehow from whatever he sensed lurking behind her father's eyes.

* * *

Ten days before his trip, Aaron had a meeting with his faculty adviser to discuss his fall writing project. He had an unsettled feeling as he settled into the wooden chair across from Professor Allen in an office that was a jumbled mess of academia. Law books lined the shelves behind the professor's desk, and several volumes lay in piles on chairs and small tables around the room. The sturdy walnut desk was littered with stacks of papers, more books, and an overflowing inbox, but it wasn't the clutter that troubled Aaron. He felt a kind of anxious quality wafting from the professor. Beneath his furrowed brow, the man's eyes seemed uneasy, unable to land on any specific spot for longer than a second.

"So what kind of progress have you made on your topic, young man?" the professor barked.

Aaron couldn't help but think of a Pekingese dog yapping as the man spoke. He almost laughed out loud at the thought, but he held himself in check and simply responded, "I've done almost all of the research and plan to start writing this weekend. I think I'm pretty much on schedule and hope to get the paper completed a few days early."

"Remind me again of your topic," Dr. Allen said.

"I'm writing about prostitution and human trafficking and the laws that try to curb these crimes."

"What an unusual topic," the professor said, shifting slightly in his seat. "And you've done your research, you say?"

"Yes, sir."

"You found enough material on the subject?"

"Yes, I think so."

"All right then. Please make an appointment if you need to discuss this with me further. You may go," said the professor, turning his attention to the stack of papers to his right.

Aaron was a little surprised by the way the professor brushed him aside. He quietly rose from his chair and left the room.

Since he had carried all of his research notes with him, expecting that Dr. Allen would want to look at them, Aaron decided to stop on the steps outside the building and go through some of the material. Besides, he loved the view of the campus from this spot with the manicured grounds and old trees. He sat down on the smooth, worn stone of the top step and pulled out his folders. Before he started to thumb through the pages, he noticed a young woman standing near the far pillar, leaning against the white marble. She wore a short red skirt and a matching polka dot blouse, which stood out in stark contrast to the background. Her hair fell in soft golden ringlets around her face and down her back. She seemed awfully young to be in college.

Aaron loved to study people and imagine their lives, so he indulged himself for a few moments. As he regarded her more closely, he discerned a kind of sadness about her. She had the look of some lost waif waiting for a rescuer. He imagined she might be literally lost on a sprawling campus, perhaps a new student who hadn't quite managed to get the lay of the land yet.

As he pondered her situation, Aaron heard the door behind him close and turned to see Professor Allen exiting the building. The man walked directly toward the young blonde. Aaron thought at first she might be his daughter or maybe even his granddaughter, but her demeanor said otherwise. She giggled when he approached, then leaned in and whispered something into the man's ear. He, in turn, put an arm around her waist, and from this angle Aaron saw him run a hand down to the small of her back and then lower. She giggled again. Likely remembering where he was, the professor regained a sense of decorum and nudged her aside. They walked down the steps with at least a foot between them and then left in the direction of the parking lot.

Aaron now understood the uneasy sense he had earlier in the professor's office. It was all too clear why he was given the brushoff even though his appointment had been scheduled for some time. Aaron couldn't help wondering about the lost girl. That was how he would think of her now.

Chapter 14

Edvin Karlsson made two to three trips per month with his new colleague and friend Axel. Although he enjoyed Axel's company, the driving became tiresome since they arrived home early in the morning with little sleep and had to prepare for work the next day.

The girls they transported were usually pretty good looking but remained quiet and usually slept in the rear seat. Edvin tried to start a conversation to pass the time.

"Are you planning a career in moving pictures or just modeling?" he asked.

"Yes, pictures are my dream," the young woman said. "But I will get some exposure as a model first."

He thought they were exceptionally young and naïve. What kind of assurance had they been given? *And what happens*, he thought to himself, *when their hopes and dreams are dashed as inevitably they will be?*

"Do your parents know about this training?" he asked.

Upon hearing this sensitive question, Axel cleared his throat and made a slight but noticeable motion with his hand. "Not a good topic," he whispered.

Edvin was never paid, but he was always promised a lump sum someday.

The usual routine was broken on one trip when one young lady brought excitement to their journey. She walked with a lively step and a slight sway to her body and greeted them with a big smile and a friendly handshake.

"What brings you to this training program?" Edvin inquired.

"You want to know my business?" she replied as she swung her legs up and over Edvin's seat, pulling her dress up and pointing to her crotch. "This is my business right here."

"How much are you charging us today?" Axel asked.

"No charge today and we shall be friends forever," she answered.

With that, Axel swung the car over to the side of the road, put his arm around her, and led her to a tall grassy area about 20 yards away. Not wasting any time, he kneeled over her, pulling off her clothes.

Edvin followed Axel as he usually did. Exhausted and smiling, they all got back in the car.

This was a milestone in their relationship. Starting that day, Axel felt closer to Edvin and free to disclose more details about his sideline.

Sitting down later at their favorite table in the pub, Axel spoke in a somewhat hushed voice as he began to explain his little satellite business.

"A couple of years ago, a man came to me and said he was a messenger representing a multinational corporation. He offered me the opportunity to make money in a sideline enterprise which involved picking up teenage girls at their home or a disclosed location and bringing them to another location. It sounded like a taxi service. Since you joined in with me, you now know exactly what it was.

"More recently I pressed that messenger to tell me more about these girls and where they go and what they do. He described a worldwide organization active in just about every major city in the world in which young girls are enlisted to carry out services for men who are in high positions and will treat them with great respect. Many of the services are sexual. These girls, mostly Chinese, are told that this is just a temporary activity leading to big, important jobs in the entertainment industry and that they will someday become famous and rich. These girls come from poor homes and have been given very little, so the offer sounds to them like a dream come true. Of course, it's not true and they get tired of being a prostitute. If they try to escape, they are punished severely. A man by the name of Victor Wong is an executive who is responsible for the operations and finances in our area. Victor will be happy to meet you but only if you have at least one young lady who you think is a candidate for our enterprise. If you do have such a lady, then he will help you get things started." Axel's eyes wore an eager, greedy expression as he stared at Edvin intently.

Edvin indeed had a young lady in mind. She was the daughter of a couple who worked at the mill. She was mentally retarded but attractive and pleasant. Her underdeveloped faculties left her unable to take care of herself.

"I know of someone," Edvin said without sharing any details about her. "Her parents might agree to placing her with people who would look after her welfare and where she could earn plenty of money."

"With Victor's help, I found a large home in a secluded wooded area outside of Helsingborg,"

Axel said. "I think she would be comfortable there. I have a nice room waiting for another *guest*. My brother, who is a fair cook, is in charge of the place and could keep an eye on her and make sure she gets taken care of."

Axel continued, "You may wonder where we would find customers for these young ladies. There are many German officers in the area. Some are in charge of procuring agricultural products including those from Mr. Bowles' dairy for the army. They make purchases and schedule the deliveries. A young Army officer named Adrian Becker is in charge of keeping the army properly supplied. There are also some well-mannered German officers there. All I have to do is offer a young lady's services to one or two of them. They are pleased to have such a chance, and, of course, spread the word to their colleagues. These Germans are away from home and miss their wives and girlfriends. In a short time, I was making a lot of money. You might even say I am getting rich even while sharing some of my profits with Victor.

"You may be wondering how you can do the same. You'll see if you can identify just one lady to join in. There's plenty of room in my house, and my brother can handle more ladies. You can have a chance to become a wealthy man like me."

Edvin's response was short and sweet. "Thanks for offering all of this to me, Axel. I will certainly think about it."

The two stood up and parted ways.

Later that day, Axel thought about his meeting with Edvin and tried to recollect the expressions on his face in order to get a feeling for how interested he might be. One thing that disturbed Axel was the guilt he felt about these young women. He always thought of them as poor souls who totally had lost their freedom and were forced into a form of slavery. He felt ashamed, yet his impoverished circumstances led him to believe that he had a right to do what he needed to rise beyond that state. He was shocked, though, that Edvin showed essentially no sign of guilt or shame when confronted with the idea of procuring young women. He had no comments or questions along those lines. Maybe Edvin was a lucky man to be able to do something like this without feeling guilty.

Chapter 15

Edvin had thoughts of his own after their conversation. He believed himself to be superior to Axel and, therefore, the rightful leader of the pair. From the very beginning of their relationship, he had displayed leadership, teaching him and presenting the ideas, and that's the way he wanted it. Edvin was not one to follow, not in the long run. He believed that he was stronger and more intelligent than Axel and, therefore, the natural leader of the two.

He visualized a number of new German clients with money to spare and a group of reasonably attractive young women, a combination that was sure to make him a wealthy man. He gave little thought to how he would find suitable girls, but fate was kind and soon handed up to him a couple on a silver platter.

"Hello, this is a Swedish citizen calling. Is this the mayor's office in Holstein? Oh, yes, very good. I've heard about the efforts here to quickly identify all the Jewish families in Denmark for transport to Sweden. I have suddenly recalled a Jewish family on the outskirts of Copenhagen.

They are farmers living in a rural area, and, as such, they are not well known."

"Yes, we know about them. Nevertheless, we thank you for your efforts to help. They are the Zielinski family, a mother, father, teenage son, and two young teenage girls. Is that the family you have in mind?"

"Yes, that's the one I had in mind. Do you need help sailing them over from Denmark?"

"We are settled in that department, but again thank you for your offer. You see they own a truck and are close enough to Highway 17. They can drive to the shore where we have made arrangements for a fishing boat to pick them up at 2:00 in the morning from wherever they find a nearby hiding place."

Edvin put the phone down with a self-satisfying smile. Now he would begin his leadership of Axel, much sooner than he expected and with a much better opportunity than he had anticipated.

"Axel, have you heard that the Christian families of Denmark are helping to rescue all the Jews by boat tonight to Sweden? It could mean a lot for us as I have some information about a farming family outside of Copenhagen with two teenage girls. There is a plan in place to pick them up somewhere near the outlet of Highway 17 around two or three in the morning. I think you should get your brother to help us. Get a fishing boat, and we shall sail over to the Danish coast somewhere near the Highway 17 area. Bring your pistol. We shall watch them load the boat secretly, follow them at a distance, and then intercept them midway and take the two girls—with force and with my gun if necessary. It will be my job to calm the parents down, assuring them that their daughters will be well treated, that they will be returned in some months with a smile and lots of money. Ask your brother to fix up another room. I know we have extra beds there. And get lots of extra food. We're on our way, Axel, to making a fortune. "

Thinking they were discovered by the Germans, the boat carrying the Zielinskis stopped without a fight. With a hood covering his face and head, Edvin explained to the sobbing mother and angry father, who were held at gunpoint, that their daughters would be kept in Sweden and would be taken care of.

Back in Sweden, Axel and his brother Lars drove the two girls, their wrists tied together, back to the house. Edvin returned to the mayor's office to make his appearance as he did wherever possible as a well-meaning Swedish citizen.

The girls were taken into a beautifully decorated house with upholstered Scandinavian furniture, deep carpets, and tables. Lars brought out wine and a feast such as the girls had never seen. After enough wine, the young women soon relaxed and told the men they were twins, 16 years old, one named Greta and the other Margo.

The men brought out new silk outfits in bright colors that were designed to show sexy, curvaceous figures. While the girls' curves were ample, bands of solid muscles trained by years of hard work on the farm showed on their forms.

The twins confessed to having had sexual experiences with some of the farm boys in their area. But neither of them had an inkling of what was to come in the days and weeks to follow.

* * *

Adrian Becker, the German supply officer, came often to the house outside Helsingborg to bring provisions for the girls. A timid but handsome young man, he spent his time there busying himself with delivering and stacking the items he procured for the house, but one day Margo came into the kitchen as he was putting away the goods he had brought. He felt drawn to her the moment he saw her and smiled in spite of his shyness. She returned his smile and greeted him warmly, something he had not expected under the circumstances. From that first meeting, they felt an instant kinship, and his trips to the house became more frequent. He found time to walk with her in the woods and even managed to steal her away for a picnic. He was in no position to help her because of his ties to Axel and Edvin, who kept a close watch on the twins. But Adrian dreamed of a day when Margo and he could have a different life.

Chapter 16

Aaron's sleep was broken that night by a series of dreams that troubled him. He had been studying for exams on property in Constitutional Law for the last 48 hours. His neck and back ached, and his eyes were getting bleary. He welcomed sleep when it came, but the dream kept repeating and woke him.

He dreamed of large rolls of paper rolling down a long hallway, heading straight for him. He had to dodge them to avoid a collision. The setting seemed to be a factory or mill. His brain kept working to recall what made a paper mill so important to him. Someone had mentioned a paper mill recently. But who?

He went back to sleep. That morning as he dressed he thought of Sara. He had a strong sense that she would understand the dream, so he arranged to see her at school as early as possible.

"Hi, Sara," he said as the two of them met in front of the library. He immediately began to share about his dream. "Listen, I dreamed all of last night something about paper, rolls of paper, maybe in a factory. Does that mean something to you?"

"Yes, of course it does. I've told you that my father is an executive for a paper company.

Years ago, before I came along, he was a supervisor in Sweden in a paper mill."

"I would like to talk with your father again. When I met him, he was in such a hurry that I barely got a chance to see what he looked like."

In truth, the flash of insight that came to Aaron in that brief meeting had chilled him, but he wanted to shield Sara from what he thought he saw. At the same time, he needed to be sure. How could he really perceive a man's character based on a fleeting glimpse?

"There's something about him and that paper mill that seems to *bother* me. Do you remember back when we first talked about a person's gaze and my ability to see some deeply held emotions within a person's eyes?"

"Yes, I do remember that. I just can't imagine how my father and his gaze would hold any special meaning for you."

"I understand that it must sound a bit crazy, but nevertheless I want to take another good, hard look at your father's face."

"I'm sure that will happen at *some* point," Sara said. "It's just...Well, he's been so strange lately and away from home a lot. I'm not certain how or when we can make that happen."

Aaron let the subject drop since he didn't want to press her when she was already feeling stressed.

Chapter 17

As far back as the night the twins were kidnapped from the boat carrying them from Denmark to Sweden, Lars had a special interest in these two young ladies. They were not particularly pretty, but they had joyful personalities and lovely smiles, and they directed their remarks mostly to him because he was closer to them in age.

In the months that followed, Lars acted like a gentleman, giving the two girls their meals, cleaning their room, and running all kinds of errands for them. He was, in fact, their jailkeeper, but they didn't see it that way. They believed that, when the time was right, they would escape or somebody would come for them.

On the night of his injury, Lars, who was not much of a drinker, had too much to drink and let his curiosity get the better of him. He wanted to know what they would look like without any clothes. He figured he could look at them while they were sleeping, so he sneaked into their room and stood beside Greta's bed. Crouching down close to the floor, he began to lower her blanket, raise her nightclothes, and quietly kneel down to examine the body of this teenager he liked so much.

Margo lay still in the twin bed next to her sister's. Her eyes slightly opened she caught a glimpse of Lars' movements. Stealthily, she rolled out of bed and crept silently along the wall. As she passed the fireplace, she grabbed one of the irons; holding it with two hands, she slung it over her shoulder, edged up closer to the bed, and with all her force swung the iron, aiming at the side of his head. Lars yelled out briefly and then fell quiet.

Greta awakened and jumped out of bed. The two of them grabbed as many clothes and blankets as they could hold and started running down the hallway, yelling to all the other women that they were alone and free and to leave now.

The girls ran through the wooded area guided only by the moonlight, dodging trees and bushes, and trampling small plants along the way. Dim headlights appeared ahead. Margo motioned toward the lights, and the two turned together, running out onto the road directly in front of an oncoming car, which turned out to be the patrol car of Sgt. Berrgen of the local police station.

Berrgen helped the girls into his car and listened as the two of them shared their story. He promptly called his boss, the stationmaster, to report the twins' harrowing escape and the injury to the jailkeeper in the process. Stationmaster Tegnell quietly but urgently told Berrgen to bring them into the station. He proceeded to send a doctor to bandage Lars and immediately contacted Edvin to make sure that Axel and Lars were given safe passage out of the country. Tegnell next contacted his leader in the organization, telling him that the twins and all the other young women had escaped.

"The house will have to be closed immediately and all traces of our activities erased," he said.

Following his orders, Edvin brought the other girls he had been able to round up after the twins fled to a vacant apartment in a small town outside of Paris. Although Lars was bandaged, his gash still bled and required stitches, so Edvin contacted a doctor to see to the wound once they arrived in France. The brothers were advised to wait at the apartment until they received further instructions.

Chapter 18

Prior to law school, Aaron had attained his bachelor's degree in history with a minor in political science. He always possessed a particular interest in World War II thanks to his ancestry and the stories he heard growing up. When he had extra time, which wasn't often thanks to his schedule, he pulled out a history book and dove into his favorite subject.

Late in 1944, the Allies extended the Normandy invasion into the Ardennes Forest. As they pushed East towards Germany, a severe winter with heavy snows set in. Along with a major counterattack by the Germans, the weather stopped further advancement of the Allied offensive. This would be Hitler's last offense and final attempt to block the Allies. He saw an opportunity to break into the Allied lines and, by attrition, to destroy both ends, sending them back to the coast.

The Germans ordered all available fighting units to reinforce their troops and completely force what was a bulge into a complete break. They well understood this offensive might be their last.

The small force of German soldiers in Denmark was not overlooked, and they were swiftly ordered to the front. German units in Copenhagen had been planning a firing squad to punish all of the Danish citizens caught participating in the escape of the Danish Jews; however, the personnel selected for the firing squad were now integrated into the massive push back to Belgium. Even the most high-ranking German officers now had to comply with the rush order to report with their commands to the Ardennes. As a result, they were not able to find a suitable firing squad. The only men who remained available were cooks, auto mechanics, and traffic police with minimal training in armaments.

Nevertheless, the executions were scheduled at the city hall in the main square. Six prisoners were tied to stakes. Attempting to understand the loading and firing of their rifles, the makeshift firing squad gathered in a small group, arguing and questioning how to carry out their assignment.

The town hall at the main square was comprised of a three-story building that housed offices for many agencies and administrative headquarters of the country. A clock tower loomed above the courtyard at the top of the building. The well-kept, grassy grounds below served as a gathering place for townsfolk and was even used as picnic spot on Sunday afternoons. On this occasion, it was the location for carrying out the death sentence of Danish citizens with everyone else ordered to witness their end.

Because hospital space was limited, Germans had a makeshift clinic set up in the offices and hallways to treat and provide rest to convalescing, wounded German soldiers.

That's where Aaron's grandfather and great grandfather entered the story. He had heard the tale many times. Medical staff in Sweden and Denmark had been enlisted to provide equipment and personnel as frequently as possible to treat the wounded.

Assisted by his son Jeremy, Filip Seitner was a regular participant in the clinic. His reputation as a specialist created a demand for his services for at least five to 10 days every month. Having heard warnings of the impending executions, Filip and Jeremy made their way to Copenhagen, carrying their usual equipment and medicines and bandages in large boxes. Buried underneath the equipment in these bags and boxes were two automatic rifles.

They entered the clinic and greeted everybody as usual. After getting their large boxes of equipment brought in, they retrieved what they needed and climbed the seldom used stairway leading up to the clock tower. Carrying the automatic weapons beneath their coats, they carefully made their way up the narrow stairway and onto the wooden path leading to the clock. Filip found a small open window that looked down on the site of the prisoners and the Germans. He and Jeremy positioned their weapons in the window. Because of the height of the tower, they were forced to use a 45° angle as they rested their weapons on the sill of the window. They were barely able to see their targets through the gun sights.

Filip watched as the members of the firing squad argued with one another and bumbled their way through practicing the firing and reloading their weapons. He took advantage of this confusion and gave a sign to Jeremy to begin shooting. They showered the Germans below with enough bullets to quickly bring them all down. Seeing this turn of events, the townspeople who were gathered below ran to free the prisoners, swiftly escorting them out of the square and out of sight.

Filip and Jeremy hid their weapons among the rafters and quickly retraced their steps, running back down the stairs. They donned their white clinic aprons. They were met by shouts of excitement about how the Danish prisoners, many of whom were well known, had escaped.

"All in a day's work of saving people," Filip whispered to his son.

* * *

Aaron tried to imagine his grandfather Jeremy and his great grandfather actually shooting the firing squad members. The story lived in his mind as a child each time he heard it, but, knowing Filip was a doctor dedicated to saving lives, it was difficult to reconcile his actions with his calling. Aaron surmised that in war the price of saving the lives of the innocent was sometimes ending the lives of those who persecuted them.

Chapter 19

Several months passed and the Gustafson brothers, Lars and Axel, remained in hiding in their third-floor apartment north of Paris. The wound on the younger brother, Lars, had healed and he was free of pain. The brothers had become restless and bored. They were grateful when Edvin came to check on them.

During the brothers' stay in Paris, Edvin covertly and gradually sought to become more involved in Victor Wong's organization while remaining a seemingly upstanding citizen by all outer appearances. Edvin remained in contact with Lars and Axel and arranged to travel to Paris to visit them.

Once there, he spent time with Lars and Axel to discern what their next steps might be. The three of them were surprised by Victor Wong's gentle knock on the door.

After a brief period of catching up with each other, they drew their chairs closer and lowered their voices. Victor was the first to speak.

"The war has practically destroyed Western Europe," he said. "Millions of families have been broken or destroyed through Nazi arrests and Allied bombings. Young girls all over Europe are alone and seeking shelter. This is a perfect time for us to expand our business. We should offer clean, warm housing, lots of good food, and nice clothing to the girls we select. They'll consider themselves fortunate in view of the alternate way of life facing them.

"My partners and I have decided that you two brothers will manage a new house that's being furnished now not far from here. It's big enough to house about 12 girls. If you men manage reasonably well, I can promise that by the end of the first year you will both be wealthy men. Not only that but in subsequent years your work with our organization will provide you with ever increasing wealth beyond your imagination. I'll be in touch with you again in the coming weeks. Please just relax here and keep a low profile."

Before shaking hands and making their final goodbyes, Victor quietly pulled Edvin aside and put his arm around his shoulder.

He whispered, "I want you to know that the management of our organization has been keeping their eye on you, and we feel that you have good management talent. We will be needing that in the future, so you shall be treated well, my friend, and a future will belong to you."

These words had a magnificent effect on Edvin. Since childhood, he had growing inside of him an image of himself as superior, as a true leader, not necessarily a leader of the beneficent. He found it difficult to describe his feeling. He believed if he were to make a mistake, it wasn't the same as anybody else making a mistake. In fact, it would be only natural and expected for him to point a finger at others and blame a blunder on them. Was this sinful? Not to him. Increasingly at this stage of his life, he felt his life meant more than others. It was only natural that his parents had protected the child who came to them so late in their lives and did their best to ensure his life was easy.

Since Edvin came from a Lutheran family, it could be argued that this mental state was unexpected; however, in their ignorance, his parents supported these feelings of superiority and overlooked the fact that in many ways his performance and behavior were mediocre at best.

Chapter 20

Starting in 1939 with Hitler's invasion of Poland, a great portion of the continent had been quickly forced by military might into subjugation. World War II in Europe ended in May 1945 with the unconditional surrender of Germany. The fighting stopped, and the heavy yoke of German occupation was removed. Following the war, celebrations began all over Western Europe.

Poland and most of Eastern Europe were not as fortunate in that they traded domination by Germany for the heavy hand of Russia. The German presence had been felt in Sweden and throughout most of Scandinavia; however, because of their neutrality, the killings and most of the destructive forces of the war had been avoided. Sweden's reputation as an agricultural source had been enhanced, and the country's economy began to grow.

The Svensson-Seitner Clinic had become famous as a result of their highly successful programs in practicing the most modern procedures to treat the tragically wounded civilian and military victims of the war. A few months after the war ended, the city honored the clinic, changing its name to the Swedish Center for Healing. Friends of the clinic, former patients, citizens of the city, and their loved ones were all invited to share in this proud renaming of Sweden's famous clinic. Tables were set up all over with delectable foods well known and famous in Scandinavia. Vodka from Finland was served and available to all.

Remembering that Edvin had allegedly played an important role in saving the Danish twin girls on the night of their escape, Filip welcomed Edvin as a guest. Edvin had managed to create an image of the well-meaning, respectable citizen while, in fact, he was operating a new and bigger addition to the slave trade that was growing in Europe. Guests stood around the tables of food, laughing and reminiscing in camaraderie with Filip and his wife Gabriella. She had never met Edvin, so Filip called her over to make the introductions. She approached him with a smile.

"Very happy to meet you," she said. "I have heard so much about you." As Gabriella looked into his eyes, she saw an image that deeply frightened her as it had done in times past. She tried to carry on a conversation with Edvin, but her body was trembling.

Filip thought she was becoming sick. Putting his arm around her, he escorted his wife to the outside of the dining area. She talked to Filip and try to explain what she had just seen in Edward's eyes was the presence of evil, which she'd seen before. She feared for the future of anyone in contact with Edvin. Her feelings were difficult to articulate, but she did the best she could to explain to her husband.

From where he stood, Edvin could interpret reasonably well that Gabriella was upset, trembling, and distraught. He knew that her agitated state had started when she gazed into his eyes. He maintained his outer appearance of control, something he had learned to do long ago. His intuition told him that she might mean trouble for him, that she had made some form of identification or connection with him. Whatever she was doing or thinking, it frightened him. He walked toward the nearest exit, fighting to maintain his composure. He knew that his next step was to contact Victor to request an immediate transfer to the United States.

Back home that evening, Gabriella cried and trembled and held onto Filip. "I'm sure of what I saw in his eyes," she said. "It's an ugly, evil, devilish look—one to be feared."

Chapter 21

After the Danish twins escaped from captivity, Edvin was constantly worried about being recognized. A turning point for him was the night he was introduced to the wife of the Polish clinic leader, Dr. Filip Seitner. Her reaction to him was so violent that he kept replaying it in his mind.

"Certainly, she must have recognized me. Why else would she have reacted that way?" he confessed to Victor Wong, who had no explanation for this kind of reaction but, nevertheless, attempted to calm his fears.

"How could the lady recognize you? Even if the twins had described you, how many times did they even see you, especially in your role at the house?"

Edvin agreed that his fear of this lady was irrational. "Honestly, the truth is that, to the best of my memory, Dr. Seitner's wife barely even looked at me or listened to me talk that evening but rather was completely and immediately focused on my eye."

Victor studied Edvin's demeanor as he spoke and considered his words before continuing. Finally, he said, "I would like to tell you a few things about our business that you're probably not aware of, and in so doing I will bring you up to date on how things are.

"Over the last couple of years, we have added about 20 houses across Europe and Asia. There are so many teenage girls on the streets who are abused and neglected, often lacking badly needed medical attention. They may be living with one or two parents but lack the care that is generally expected from a parent. And so they give up their life at home. They turn to prostitution, drugs, and the company of men who deceptively convince them that they have a better life to offer. So they are captured and sold like a wild animal. You might say to be imprisoned in a life of serving men as prostitutes or maybe home cleaners or some other menial job. They bring in enormous profits for the man who owns them.

"And now something that would interest you a great deal. There are very few arrests among our many colleagues. You see we support each other and help each other with legal problems when and if they come up. In fact, there have been very few arrests and convictions, and, when we have them, the penalty is very light.

With our combined wealth, we have the means to offer would-be accusers a reason to stay silent.

"What I envision for you is a management position in a paper mill somewhere in the greater New York area. We would maintain one or two houses close by so that you could spend simply one or two nights a week seeing to your side business. I am even now exploring possibilities for you.

"Edvin, your future is secure. Our organization likes you and will build increasing trust in you, and, of course, there will be a lot of money coming your way.

"There is a term now used by the law and the media which is 'human trafficking.' Sounds like a terrible crime that we are committing, but there is very little interference by the law enforcing people. We have many influential friends and a great deal of money to support them. Our protection is guaranteed for many years, so just relax!"

Wong's vision for Edvin soon would become realized through the many participants in the trafficking industry to be found throughout most of North America. The war left many children without parents and without homes, so the traffickers who promised a comfortable life with food and shelter, asking only for sex or hard

work as repayment lured many unfortunates
into servitude.

Chapter 22

As Wong drove away from his meeting with Edvin, he had some second thoughts about perhaps promising too much. After all, how well did he know the man? Was he getting lost in the strong desire that he and his colleagues in the upper echelons of his business had for middle management, seemingly respectable people to drive their business? He must not allow his zeal to override his discernment and neglect his need to evaluate those that would be an asset and those that would *not* be.

So he began to ponder some previous incidents where he had a chance to perceive the man's character. One thing that stood out in his mind was the fact that Edvin never took any responsibility when things went wrong. Although it was true that Edvin was a remarkably efficient man who knew how to get things done, Edvin never seemed to find any fault in his own actions. Was this an extreme of his personality?

Wong's mind revolved around some of the situations where difficulties had arisen and recognized that he hadn't thought twice about the fact that Edvin was never wrong—at least in his own opinion. Wong began to see that this was a man who made decisions based on nothing more than his own will and who seemed to possess an absence of values and an absence of submission to any higher being.

Wong was unable to deal with the concept of how evil might be influencing his colleague now or in the future. Although he could not see it, Wong and Edvin were deeply similar. A world of evil or bad choices did not exist for either of them. Wong lacked the ability to look deeply into his own conscience nor could he imagine Edvin looking there either.

Chapter 23

After a productive weekend writing his paper, Aaron felt good about his progress and decided to meet Sara for their usual Monday lunch study session instead of working more on the term writing project. Sara looked particularly appealing in her soft pink cashmere sweater and gray pencil skirt. Aaron often imagined a time when they might become closer.

Sara sat down next to him in the noisy dining hall, positioning her heavy satchel containing a notebook and law books beside her on the empty seat to her left.

"I skipped breakfast and I'm starving. Will you hold our spots while I go grab something to eat?"

Having already gotten a tray with lunch, Aaron was happy to oblige. Sara returned quickly and the two of them ate in silence before tackling their briefs for criminal law. Aaron sensed Sara's mind was on something other than her studies or her lunch, so as she swallowed her last bite, he took the opening and asked.

"Oh, I'm fine," she said, but her face told a different story.

To Aaron's gaze, she seemed out of sorts and moody. He peered intently into her eyes, which made her squirm noticeably.

"Oh, all right, Aaron. You certainly have a way of prying things out of me without saying a word.

"My parents had a huge argument this morning. My father stays out late night after night, supposedly for work, although who knows why a paper company would require his attention at *those* hours. My mother is usually pretty meek about things, but I guess she'd had enough after he had been out so many late nights and then being away almost all weekend. She wouldn't back down this time, and he…he…he almost hit her. I saw him pull back his hand, and the look in his eyes—"

Aaron reached out and gently touched her forearm. He recalled that man's eyes and easily could envision the scene. He wished he had some words of wisdom to make things better, but he could think of nothing useful.

"I'm sorry," he said. "Is there anything I can do?"

She looked up from the table and said, "Just be my friend. If you weren't around, well, let's just say I'm thankful for a friend long about now."

Without thinking, he blurted out an invitation. "Look, I'm going home to visit my parents for the high holidays. I'm leaving Friday morning. Do you want to come with me? I haven't asked them, but I'm sure my mother would welcome you if you don't mind going to temple on Saturday night for the Rosh Hashanah service, or I guess you could stay at the apartment while we go."

Sara appeared surprised by the suggestion but nonetheless answered quickly. "I'd love to," she said. "Getting away would be kind of perfect right now.

"There's just one thing," she added. "I'll have to clear it with my parents, and my father's absences will be even more noticeable if I'm away. I'll let you know tomorrow for sure. Okay?"

After they went their separate ways for the rest of the day, the two of them shared the news with both sets of parents, and plans were made for Sara to join Aaron on his trip home.

* * *

Aaron escorted Sara into his parents' townhouse apartment on Connecticut Avenue. Their place had only one guest bedroom, which would be occupied by Aaron's paternal grandparents for the holidays, so Sara stayed in Aaron's room, and he took the sofa. His mother had already cleared space for her things in the closet and one of the drawers.

Sara was as charming as ever when she met his mother, who greeted them upon their arrival. Aaron's father had gone to pick up his own parents from the airport. Gabriella and Filip Seitner seldom traveled anymore, but the high holidays and family enticed them to leave Sweden.

"Sara, we look forward to having you for Shabbat dinner tonight. Why don't you get settled and then have some rest this afternoon? We have quite a schedule of events this weekend."

By the time Sara rose from her nap, Aaron's grandparents had arrived, and his mother and grandmother were busily preparing dinner in the kitchen while Aaron sat with his father and grandfather in the living room. They greeted Sara warmly when she came downstairs and was introduced.

Smells of challah baking, soup simmering, and brisket being reheated wafted from the kitchen and roused Aaron's appetite.

"I should probably go in to help your mother and grandmother," Sara suggested.

Aaron's father grinned. "That's really kind, Sara," he said, "but there's no room for another cook when those two are in the kitchen."

As sundown drew close, they gathered around the dining table. Sara was briefly introduced to

Gabriella as she and Anna prepared the table for Shabbat, but Aaron's grandmother paid little attention given her focus was on the meal to come. Finally, the candles were lit, the wine and challah were blessed, and everyone was ready to eat.

Aaron and Sara were seated across from his grandparents, and his father and mother took their places at the ends of the table. Aaron wondered how his grandmother would react to Sara. She was, after all, the one who passed on his gift of gazing into the eyes to discern what lay behind them. As he recalled from years past, conversation was lively around the dinner table whenever his parents and paternal grandparents were together, and there was no shortage of catching up to do despite the fact that they spoke by phone and wrote letters to one another.

As the meal wound down and the candles burned low, the wine and the heavy meal began to make Aaron feel drowsy. He regretted not napping after the long train ride and found himself yawning.

Finally, his grandmother, the one and only Gabriella Seitner, counselor and wise advisor, turned her attention to the young woman opposite her.

"Tell me about your family, young lady," she said. "I believe my grandson said you're from Sweden."

"My parents are," Sara replied. "My father is from Halmstad, and my mother grew up in Gothenburg before her parents moved to the United States. I was born here."

Aaron watched as his grandmother fixed her gaze on Sara, peering deeply into her eyes as she spoke.

"What are their names? Not that we would know them, of course, but you seem somehow oddly familiar to me," Gabriella Seitner said. "And, of course, we encountered so many people during the war."

Aaron thought a touch of some remote sorrow passed over his grandmother's face as her eyes were drawn into the distance and memories seemed to color her countenance in the stain of past pain. When she looked back at them, Sara captured her focus again.

"Garland and Elsa Knight," Sara replied.

"That doesn't sound like a Swedish name," his grandmother persisted.

"Oh, no, ma'am, you're right. My father changed his name to sound more American and fit in here better at the paper company he manages. He was actually born Edvin Karlsson."

The blood seemed to drain from his grandmother's face for a moment. She was a force of nature and one of the strongest people Aaron knew. He couldn't imagine her looking so shaken until he saw it happen.

His grandmother brought her hands from her lap to rest on the table in front of her and bent forward slightly.

"Look into my eyes, girl," she said.

Sara shifted uneasily in her chair. "I don't understand."

"Look into my eyes," his grandmother repeated.

Sara leaned forward. Even from his view beside her, Aaron could see the candlelight dancing in her eyes. He knew exactly what his grandmother was doing. She was going to read those eyes as he had done in the restaurant.

His grandmother remained silent as her gaze bored into Sara. At last she said, "I've seen those eyes before. You have your father's eyes. But they are also your own. Only a shadow of him lives in your eyes."

"You know my father?" Sara said, stunned. "But how? And what do you mean? What shadow?!"

Aaron noticed his grandmother's hands shaking as she withdrew them back below the table. She said nothing for a few moments.

"I think I need to lie down," she spoke at last. "Anna, I hate to leave the clearing of the table to you, but I need to rest. I regret to say that the long flight and dinner preparations have exhausted me. I hope you understand."

"Of course," Anna said.

"Mother, can I help you?" Jeremy asked.

"No, I'll be all right. I just need to lie down."

Aaron's grandfather stood and helped his wife up from her chair and to the guest bedroom upstairs.

Sara was clearly shaken from the experience with his grandmother, so Aaron invited her to return to the living room.

"I should really help your mother clear the table and wash the dishes."

Anna said, "That's quite all right, Sara. You're our guest. Please spend some time with Aaron. I'm sorry for the sudden end to dinner. I think we may all want to retire early tonight."

Once they were seated on the sofa, Aaron put a hand on Sara's arm and whispered, "Are you okay?"

Sara's brow was pinched, and Aaron thought he saw a tear threatening to emerge from the corner of her eye.

"What did I do wrong? I don't understand. What did your grandmother see?"

"I'm sorry, Sara. She rarely reads people in that way anymore, but I guess she saw some kind of connection to your father." Aaron really did not want to say more. He had never divulged what her eyes revealed to him when he turned his gaze to her in the restaurant. Sara was her own person, but something of her father existed in her too. If she pressed him, Aaron had no idea what he would tell her.

Thankfully, Sara seemed ready to brush the incident aside. He supposed she had her own suspicions about her father's innermost being. How could she *not*? Although he detected a lurking somber tone about her demeanor, Aaron chose to ignore it. Sara went to bed, and everyone let the matter drop amidst the activities of the Jewish new year.

Chapter 24

Many of the thousands of Europeans who survived the war found it impossible to return to their earlier lives as their homes had been reduced to bombed-out shells or taken over by strangers. Jewish communities no longer existed throughout much of Europe. Many survivors became displaced persons and were forced to live in camps under military occupation. There they waited to be admitted to the United States or Palestine. Initially, with old immigration policies, the number of refugees admitted was greatly limited. This was particularly true with Palestine under the control of the British government. In 1946, the total number of Jewish displaced persons was about 250,000, which included survivors of the Holocaust.

In 1947, the United Nations voted to partition Palestine into two new states, one Jewish and the other Arab. About six months later, the State of Israel was formed. Jewish immigration into the new state was unrestricted, and by 1951 almost 700,000 Jews had immigrated to Israel, where they found homes and a chance to start life over principally as farmers in established settlements (kibbutzim). The first of these was Kibbutz Degania Alef, which was established in 1909 near the Sea of Galilee. Many similar settlements sprang up across the area. The land near the sea was both swampy and rocky, and the pioneer settlers endured backbreaking labor to make the soil suitable for agriculture. With limited fighting equipment, these same settlers soon battled against far superior Syrian forces with tanks and troops.

The creation of the state of Israel in May 1948 led to a series of conflicts between Arabs and Jews with much bloodshed and many deaths. The first of these started just days after the official creation of the new state. Egypt, Iraq, Transjordan, and Syria invaded the new state and fought the Israelis. They were supported by the Arab Liberation Army and corps of volunteers from Saudi Arabia, Lebanon, and Yemen. The Arab armies mounted offense on all fronts: Egyptian forces invaded from the south, Jordanian and Iraqi forces from the east, and Syrian armies attacked from the north.

Chapter 25

When Aaron's parents and grandparents gathered, the family always found time for the retelling of their history, and that weekend during Sara's visit was no exception. His parents' journey was a tale of exceptional bravery and daring. Aaron's father shared the account of his and Anna's escape from Kraków and the from Gdansk, a harrowing ordeal that Aaron's mother preferred not to relive. She left the room for a few minutes while his father related that story.

Exhausted both mentally and physically from their narrow escape from the Germans, Jeremy and his wife Anna rested and regained their strength. They shared their exciting stories with the family, ate some good food, and slept a lot. But there was work to be done. The new clinic, a combined practice of two successful doctors, had additional space that needed to be converted into examination rooms and a few hospital overnight stay rooms for the critically ill. Jeremy got involved in the new construction and helped to set up new patient procedures as there were many who, until now, with government supplied medical aid, had never been treated by a professional doctor.

Anna took nursing courses at local hospitals and found many practical applications. Months passed while Jeremy and Anna were completely involved in the clinic.

As the war in Europe ended, the Jewish settlements in Palestine became increasingly active. Through newspapers, friends, radio, and their synagogue, Jeremy and Anna maintained contact with the news from Palestine. As 1946 approached, the couple found that they still shared the dream of returning and building the new homeland for the Jews. They learned of the amazing growth rate of the settlements in Israel; most attractive to them was Kibbutz Degania, the biggest and most developed. They felt their skills in nursing and medicine and in setting up procedures, manpower allocations, and general management would be their best contribution. So they set out once again for the long trip to Palestine and Kibbutz Degania. They found themselves excited and optimistic about their future in Palestine. This would finally be their chance to dedicate their lives to the new state. The future of the Middle East, however, was still fraught with troubles and uncertainty.

The Syrian attack on Kibbutz Degania began at dawn on May 20, 1948. With a force comprised of tanks, armored cars, and infantry, the Syrians began shelling the center of the kibbutz.

A defense position on the outer perimeter of Degania was held by 70 men who were forced out of their positions quickly as Syrian tanks and troops broke through the outer fence.

Jeremy and Anna were assigned battle positions in anticipation of the attack from Syria. She carried a large briefcase with bandages, drugs, and medical equipment to treat the wounded. She would maintain a clinic in a portion of the main dining room where tables were moved to hold the wounded and dead. Jeremy carried a rifle and an allocation of ammunition. His job was to patrol the main dining room area and attempt to pick off individual Syrian soldiers who might be brave enough to enter the area. The Israeli defenders awaited delivery of new field artillery pieces promised from Tel Aviv; these were their main hope of surviving the battle. Not to be fully realized, they got by with the limited arms they could scrounge together in an astonishingly short time. After a battle of about one hour, the Syrian forces finally retreated, leaving the Israelis to care for their wounded and dead.

Leading a team of people assigned to help the wounded, Anna carried a bag of instruments and bandages from room to room, responding to cries of pain. Several Arab soldiers broke into the dining area and started to wave their comrades forward but were gunned down as they entered.

The leader of the assault was mainly interested in bringing terror to as many locations as possible. After the Syrian retreat, Jeremy counted 10 people wounded and three dead.

Anna was among the wounded, having sustained a bullet wound to her leg. Weakened from loss of blood, she was carried to an open truck with two other seriously wounded people. They were bound for the Sheba Medical Center in Tel Aviv which at that time was modestly comprised of a few old military tents. Jeremy openly positioned himself in the truck with a clear view of enemy stragglers they might encounter along the way.

Some of the wounded would remain at home to be cared for by the kibbutz medical team until a doctor arrived.

The ride to Tel Aviv was dark and bumpy. Jeremy was thankful that Anna was still alive, but she had lost a lot of blood. He was aware that this was their second attempt to join the kibbutz, and both times led to danger. He was determined now to join the fight for Jewish freedom and independence. He would be joining large numbers of Jews, many of whom had only recently been freed from German concentration camps.

No one spoke over the entire trip to Tel Aviv. Jeremy glanced over to Anna occasionally and found her sleeping and breathing quietly.

He looked out into the darkened desert while gripping his rifle. He prayed silently to a deity that had promised this land to the Jews thousands of years ago.

Chapter 26

After surgical removal of the bullet from Anna's leg, Jeremy discussed her condition with her nurse Hannah Levy. Fortunately, the bullet she took during the Syrian attack missed her bones, and she sustained a flesh wound only; however, she was weakened by a large loss of blood and a slight infection. He followed her recovery through daily visits and conversations with Hannah, a tall, strong-looking woman of about 35 who, in spite of her large feet and overall size, was relatively agile and fast.

Hannah had been on duty for 10 to 12 hours per day, caring for more patients than ever before—all of them injured in the fighting. With great care, she was able to stop the bleeding and control the infection, and, after a few days, Anna was able to sit up and converse with visitors and especially with Hannah.

"I have been thinking," Hannah said one day. "When you are fully recovered, you might want to join us here as a nurse or nurses' helper. Your experience in your father-in-law's clinic in Sweden and your efforts at the kibbutz are a wonderful foundation for you to pursue nursing more seriously."

Hannah had touched on a profound desire in Anna's mind. She wanted to be more than an assistant; she aspired to have a profession that would be hers forever so she could be an important contributor to Israel. Hannah and her staff were dedicated and would no doubt take a few minutes here and there to explain and show a particular procedure. She would definitely learn a lot that way, and she noticed that occasionally they gave some courses in nursing.

On one of Jeremy's visits to see her during her recovery, Anna had a chance to discuss this choice with him. In her mind, she felt the decision had already been made, but she wanted him to understand how much becoming a full-fledged nurse meant to her.

After listening to her describe her desire to follow a meaningful path for her life, Jeremy said, "I can tell how much this means to you. It might mean that we have to be apart some of the time though. I feel honor bound to help our country too."

Anna looked out the window at the sunlight spreading its beams onto the grounds outside. "We both have to follow our hearts, my love," she said. "I feel an urgency, a kind of inner calling, to do this just as you do to protecting and helping Israel."

He gazed into her eyes and said, "Then, it's settled. We'll follow our callings and always find our way back to each other."

Anna felt relieved and grateful. "Here's to finding our way back—always," she said.

After a few more days of rest, Anna recovered completely. She could walk and even run if she had to. She was ready to begin her career as a "nurse in training."

"You are entering a profession that, here in Israel, has a history that goes back thousands of years," Hannah proudly exclaimed as she began to teach Anna about the pioneering nurses in the region.

"In biblical times, or perhaps I should say many thousands of years ago, Moses' mother Jochebed and sister Miriam were known as Shifra and Puah, the two midwives who saved the children of the Israelites from genocide. Shifra, which means improvement, referred to Jochebed's practice of cleaning and caring for babies that were just born. Puah translates to "cooing," which refers to the sounds Moses' sister made to help newborn babies relax in their first hours of life.

"We hold the memory of Selma Mair in our hearts and minds as she came here from Germany where she was a pioneer in the study of nursing in 1962. She mastered hospital procedures and medical standards which elevated our hospitals to modern practice, which has made them some of the best in the world.

"I will tell you more of our founding women in nursing here in Israel sometime in the future. Let me just say now that we are very, very proud of our traditions."

Anna enjoyed hearing about the tradition of nursing in her new country. She felt connected to the past here more than at any time in her life and absorbed Hannah's teachings about their history.

When Anna was able to leave the hospital's care, she joined Jeremy in the residence he had secured during her hospitalization. Something had been weighing on him for quite a while, and now that he and his wife were able to find some private time, he shared his disappointment in the failure of new rifles to be delivered to the kibbutz.

"I'm going to look for the office of supplies here in Tel Aviv to investigate the problem. Something just seems off about this delay."

Anna and Jeremy were registered as Tel Aviv citizens of importance to the defense. They were given a small apartment with minimal furniture.

Chapter 27

Because of their heavy workload, they were rarely in the apartment together.

To the casual observer, Anna appeared to be a full-fledged nurse who cared for Israeli soldiers wounded in action. Jeremy spent most of his working hours trying to sort out and organize supply chains. He talked to generals and other superior officers regarding their needs and locations ideally suited for shipments. He fed this critically important information back to his counterparts in New York. He felt good to be part of a vital team.

One night, Anna and Jeremy sat quietly at dinner, staring at the food and then at each other. They came here to be farmers and to work alongside other young Zionists. Their new lives were not at all what they had envisioned, but their professions were exciting and, of course, important. Little did they know at that time how significant their contributions would become to the growth and stability of this new nation.

Schmuel Kantor surprised them with a visit the next morning, bringing Jeremy a special assignment that required travel to a small nation in North Africa. They claimed to have badly needed Spitfire airplane replacement parts for sale to Israel. Because the country was considered an unknown entity with no past dealings, it would be necessary for someone on the staff to visit and confirm the viability of the small nation as a supplier. Jeremy was given this mission. His preparation included an airline ticket, a one-night hotel reservation, some cash, and a gun along with a one-hour pass at a local shooting range.

After preparations were completed, Jeremy left on the trip. Upon arriving at his hotel, he received a packet with instructions regarding where and when to meet, a small map, and a roughed-out agenda. He had never undertaken an assignment like this and felt both honored by the trust his government placed in him and at the same time somewhat anxious about the task at hand. He paced the room for a while as he waited for the meeting's appointed time to arrive.

Finally, he made his way out of the hotel and found a taxi that could take him to the meeting place. He stood in front of a large building that once had been white, but age and weather made it appear worn and sallow. He took a deep breath before entering, mustering his confidence for the mission.

Jeremy entered a large open hall with faded blue, aqua, and white tile flooring and limestone and stucco covered walls. Straight ahead he found a pleasant-looking woman who greeted him and ushered him to a doorway into an office space. Three men sat waiting for him there. The one behind a desk offered him a seat, and all three smiled in welcome. They appeared courteous and friendly but businesslike. The man in charge offered Jeremy a glass of water from a nearby pitcher, but he declined, thinking it best to get down to business.

"Ah, yes, you'll want to see the merchandise," said the man behind the desk. "Please follow me."

Jeremy noticed that after he stood the man's pants appeared to retain a perfect crease.

Jeremy and the other two men followed him through a door at the back of the office and along a hallway that opened onto a large interior room. Tables filled with airplane parts were arranged for easy viewing throughout the expansive space. Jeremy began to inspect the parts, which appeared to be in fairly good shape.

"If you're satisfied, perhaps we could return to more a comfortable spot," the man in charge said.

Jeremy nodded and all four of them walked back the way they came. They proceeded to discuss the price and delivery options for the parts. The governmental officials appeared anxious to convert the parts into payment. Delivery details would be sent directly to Israel. The men shook hands in anticipation of a business arrangement worth a great deal to both parties.

As the meeting broke up, Jeremy found a phone and called his contact in Israel to confirm that the discussions had taken place. Details of the meeting were not mentioned. No one expected things to go smoothly. The Israeli government would be content to receive the parts albeit with new demands from the sellers.

Jeremy gently shrugged his shoulders as he thought of all the possibilities. He decided to explore the central plaza of the city where he found trays of fruit and some vegetables he had never seen before. In addition to getting something to eat, he purchased a lightweight evening gown in bright colors for Anna.

He walked back to his hotel, retrieved his key from the clerk, and then went up to his room through an old-fashioned elevator. When he entered the room, he threw his packages on the bed and walked over to the lamp between the beds to switch on the light. As he turned it on, Jeremy caught a glimpse of movement to his left and instantly looked over to see a native with a turban-wrapped head pointing a gun at him. Jeremy quickly dropped down between the two beds and pulled out his gun. The intruder took two steps directly toward his location on the floor and started to squeeze the trigger. A shot rang out and the intruder fell dead. Jeremy looked up to see a third man holding a smoking gun, a man he recognized as a security guard from his office.

Jeremy felt his heart throbbing, and he could barely call out a welcome. "I am so happy you could join us today," he said.

"Thanks," the guard said. "I think things got hot just a little sooner than I expected; nevertheless, it looks like we can bring you back in one piece."

"Sounds like you were kind of expecting some trouble here today."

"The Arabs have spies all over and hear about practically every deal that comes our way. Remember this is their part of the world. They are well-positioned in every square foot of it. All we can do now is go ahead with the steps outlined in your meeting—this time using better security. If there's a deal in the making, and I suspect there is, this will be your first successful trade. The British maintained Spitfire bases in several North African locations, and these people have found the inventory of spare parts in one or more of those. As for the guy on the floor, we don't know who sent him, and we frankly don't care. We want the parts; the details don't matter. Let's get out of here and head home."

Chapter 28

In the coming years, whether at peace or during war, Jeremy worked his way up the ranks within the government. Gradually, he moved away from supplying weaponry and military parts and more into agriculture, which was his primary interest. His responsibilities included providing food for the growing nation. He learned how to source wheat, fresh meat, and a variety of agricultural products. He even got involved in obtaining high-quality seeds and agricultural know-how. As the years flew by, he enjoyed an increasing reputation as someone who knew how to get the job done.

Anna continued to take courses while working as a nurse and eventually graduated from the Sheba Academic School of Nursing. She became pregnant and gave birth in 1950 to a healthy little boy whom she and Jeremy named Aaron after the biblical character.

The United States government became increasingly aware of the need to form close bonds with the nations of the Middle East in the areas of agriculture and industrialization. The U.S.

State Department kept lines of communication open to promote peace in the region. Jeremy and his young family were selected to take an office in Washington, D.C., to lead a joint effort in maintaining and establishing high standards of agriculture and nutrition throughout the Middle East. They were given a modest but comfortable apartment on Connecticut Avenue with convenient travel to Jeremy's office and to Anna's nursing activities in the local hospitals.

While growing up in the District of Columbia, Aaron became proficient in the English language, and his fine scholarship led eventually to an undergraduate degree in pre-law and finally to one of the best law schools on the East Coast.

* * *

Aaron always marveled at the life his parents and grandparents had led. He was glad Sara had been able to visit and hear some of the tales of their courage and commitment to helping the country of their hearts. He was thankful for the break from law school and the time with those he loved most in the world. He only wished they could have stayed longer.

The rest of fall semester sped by, and their relationship steadily grew closer. He went home again at the end of the term and got to spend

Channukah with his parents. When he returned to school after the holiday break, he and Sara shared a number of classes and continued to study together as often as possible.

Somehow, another visit with her father never seemed to happen, and Aaron noticed that Sara seemed to shut down and become distant whenever Garland Knight was mentioned. He tried time and again to get her to open up about her home life, but she remained reticent until the end of the spring term.

Chapter 29

The war in Europe ended on May 8, 1945, with the surrender of Axis Powers. In April of that year, approximately 1.5 million Axis prisoners were taken. Although hostilities had ended, townspeople all over Europe were anxious to take their own revenge on their German captors. In their failed attempt to rule the world with a Third Reich, the Nazis left a world overcome by death and destruction. The Nazis were denied a victory against Russia as a major winter storm bogged down German troops and tank advances. In the battle for Britain, a new secret weapon, radar, allowed British fighter planes to detect and destroy German bombers before they made significant penetration into the country. The discovery of the Holocaust and the Nazi attempt to slaughter Jews and thereby end their presence on earth followed, and the world was shaken by the extent of Nazi hatred against the Jews. Celebrations broke out all over Europe, and people began readjusting to their lives of freedom after years of cruel imprisonment by the Germans.

Former German soldiers who returned to their homes found a different world awaiting them. Adrian Becker, who had supplied the brothel outside Helsingborg, was shocked to discover that the Germany he remembered just a few short years earlier was gone. Now, it was a maze of bombed-out buildings and streets covered in rubble. The scene reminded him of a magician he had seen as a small boy who would hold an object in his hand, drape it with a colorful handkerchief, and then quickly pull it away, leaving his hand empty. Most public transportation was shut down. Train tracks and locomotives had been destroyed by Allied bombing. He was lucky to find a bus company that had a few vehicles still operating. One of them took him to his hometown of Kassel.

The bus ride was slow as the roads were severely damaged, and the driver frequently had to go off the shoulder in order to find a clear space to continue. After about five hours of being bounced and jerked around, Adrian stepped off the bus and contemplated what had been the downtown area of Kassel but was now essentially leveled to the ground. He tried to find his old neighborhood, but the buildings and street corners that he once used as a guide to find his home were missing. When he finally reached what he was sure was his old neighborhood, his heart sank. The homes of his neighbors, relatives, and, yes, his parents were missing. The few people he could talk to on the street told him that Allied bombing had created a literal firestorm, which, on its own, moved from street to street and building to building and demolished everything in its wake.

Adrian walked around talking to people, trying to learn the fate of his family. After an hour of combing the neighborhood, scanning the faces, and asking everyone about those he knew and loved, he finally resigned himself to the fact that everything and everyone were missing.

He found a bench in one of the city's parks and sat down for a rest. He put his head down in his hands and sobbed. The dream he had to return home and reunite with his family, to make Margo his wife, to find a new job, and begin a new life was gone. He felt lost and alone and could only see death and destruction everywhere he looked.

He and his father had neither liked nor disliked Hitler and the fascists. They had taken a wait-and-see attitude. Under such a regime, there really was no other choice.

His thoughts turned to Margo. He held the vision of her in his mind's eye, recalling the way she used to smile at him in such a warm, approving fashion. Maybe they would have learned to love each other. It was hard to tell since their beginnings evolved from such unlikely circumstances. But they would have tried. These thoughts comforted him, and he felt more relaxed.

Adrian began to realize that perhaps his future would not be in Germany but rather back in Sweden. *Nothing wrong with that*, he thought. He just wanted to be back with Margo. He began to feel more positive as he recited quietly the lines of his favorite *Schiller* poem and focused on the possibilities of the future:

> *Be embraced, Millions*
>
> *This kiss to all the world!*
>
> *Brothers above the starry canopy*
>
> *There must dwell a loving father.*
>
> *Are you collapsing, millions?*
>
> *You sense that creator, world?*
>
> *Seek him above the starry canopy!*
>
> *About the stars must he dwell.*

He thought of his future in Sweden, which could include a food store in a nice neighborhood where he would offer a wide variety of foods and drinks. After all, he knew all of the major food suppliers and their management. Certainly, they would help him at least with what they had left under these post-war circumstances. Customers would come to buy his limited stock of food items. In time, he would have more to offer and more to sell. He had some money left and thought he could afford a small store in a nice neighborhood.

He and Margo would go to Dr. Filip and ask for a recommendation as he approached the various bureaucrats in the Swedish government for permission to open a new store in a residential neighborhood of Stockholm. His heart beat faster as he began to envision this future and knew immediately he must look for fast transportation back to Stockholm and find Margo, whom he began missing even more.

So that was exactly what he did. With time and determination, Adrian found Margo and her twin sister. She agreed to marry him despite the strange circumstance of their initial meeting. Once the two of them were wed, they even secured help from a number of merchants, suppliers, and reputable sources who had known him as a kind man just trying to get by in an army he did not want to fight for.

To the manufacturers of farm products, the end of the war meant that all of the former suppliers of milk, eggs, cheese, and pork to the German Army would now be looking for buying outlets at the civilian markets throughout Scandinavia. Soon, Adrian Becker was able to open a new market with his Danish wife and her twin sister.

Because of his previous work in the German Army, Adrian had the advantage of knowing the suppliers, the quality of their goods, and their potential delivery times. He lost no time in visiting all of them and putting together deals that assured his store would carry a full line of high-quality products. His interest was less in big profits than in developing a reputation for high quality and fair business practices. His wife would assist him in tracking inventory levels. Her sister, who had become interested in doing the same with cosmetics, was contacting manufacturers in Paris who also would be looking for expanded peacetime markets. She set up a little counter in one corner of the store where she could introduce cosmetics to the stylish Swedish women who wanted to look more beautiful.

In about six months, the store grew in reputation and was full of customers most of the time, patrons who had discovered the high quality and diversity of the products sold in this market. The owners grew in pride and confidence in what they had accomplished and in their love for each other. After about a year, they were the proud parents of a little baby boy. Margo's sister Greta, who was now given frequent babysitting jobs, began to think she should start looking for a husband.

Chapter 30

As the school year ended, Aaron looked upon the summer break as an opportunity to learn more about Sara's life. Since the two of them met, they had supported each other through law school exams and papers. He was especially proud of the B+ average they had both achieved by studying together and quizzing each other throughout the spring semester.

They began to have conversations about what to do during the summer break. He still had a vague picture of her father playing an evil role in her life. He had picked up on something sinister about the man whenever she recounted small details from her childhood and adolescence. She, too, had a sense from things she picked up on that there was something true about Aaron's suspicions. She became more convinced as time went on and her father's behavior continued to prove questionable.

Aaron suggested the two of them find a way to delve into her father's dealings. Finally, he said, "I think the only way to find out more about your father would be to follow him."

"Really? That seems kind of drastic," Sara replied. Her forehead gathered into a frown as she looked off toward the university grounds.

"I seem to recall you telling me you thought he might be following you at one point."

She took a deep breath and let out a long sigh. "Yes, I did say that. I was never sure, but…" Her voice trailed off as she gazed into the distance. "I don't know," she said at last. "It just all seems so cloak and dagger."

"You're right," Aaron responded. "But how else can you really know what he's been up to when he's out of the house so much?"

After pondering for a few minutes, Sara's shoulders slumped as if resigning herself. "Okay, but he knows what our cars look like, so we can't do that. He works in the corporate office of a big paper company. How can we ever become more involved in what he does? We'd be noticed on the grounds there, and we'd stand out if we tried to follow him in either of our cars."

"We can borrow a truck," Aaron said. He had a friend who owned a truck and owed him a favor.

On the evening they decided to follow Sara's father, they waited on the opposite side of the street about 200 feet from the garage. As expected, Garland Knight exited the garage making a left turn heading along Front Street, which would lead him to the only main highway out of the city. After driving about ten miles, he signaled a right turn at the next exit. They followed him through a parking lot that extended into an open area that looked something like a softball field. They parked at a distance to avoid detection and watched as he got out of his car, walked to the main building, and then disappeared. They waited about five minutes before venturing out to head toward the house. Dusk had quickly turned to darkness, so they had to move slowly to avoid pitfalls along the way. They sneaked toward the building where he had entered. Suddenly, the path became brighter.

"Okay, you two, hold it right there," a voice spoke from the direction of the light. "See that little hut," the voice said pointing the flashlight beam toward a small shed. "Walk slowly to that hut, open the door, and sit down inside."

Neither of them could see the face of the man behind the powerful flashlight. When they arrived at the shed, he instructed them to turn their backs as he unlatched the door to the small outer building. Once it was opened, he proceeded to push them through the entrance and barked, "Sit down." As quickly as they did, he exited taking with him the only light present and closing the door. They could hear him re-latching the door from the outside.

Once seated in the shed, Aaron and Sara looked out its window toward the main structure, which appeared to be something like a motel with many lights on in rooms that spanned its five floors and an outside walkway on each floor.

As Aaron peered out the window, he saw a girl with soft golden ringlets who couldn't have been more than 16 closing the door to one of the motel rooms. She stood under the outside lights for a few moments, pulled a cigarette from her pocket, and lit it. Even at a distance, he detected a vacant look on her face. *The lost girl.* He recognized her immediately. She was the young waif who met his professor on the steps outside his office building on campus that day in September. On one of the other floors, farther from the light, he watched as a heavyset man tapped on a door. Another teenage girl came outside in response, quickly pulling the man inside.

"Did you see that, Sara?"

"I did," she said quietly. "It's really strange."

"I've seen that first girl before. She met

Professor Allen outside his office building on campus, and he was acting really oddly that day. I hate to say it, Sara, but I'm pretty sure these girls are prostitutes," Aaron said.

Sara mentally pieced together the fragments she had heard and seen since her childhood, and a most unwelcome picture began to form in her mind. "Is this what my father has been doing on those secret nights away from home?" A chill overtook her at the thought.

"Have you ever suspected anything like this?"

"I didn't know anything about sex trafficking until recently. It's shocking to think that my father..."

At that moment, the door opened, and her father stepped inside the shed, an outraged expression on his face. When he recognized his daughter, his eyes bulged in terror.

"What are you doing here, little girl?" he shouted. "Did you follow me? Have you been spying on me?!" He didn't wait for a reply. "Now you know where the money has been coming from. I have kept nothing of value from you and your mother. You have had the best money could buy including a college education and law school. And now that I have been discovered, I suppose I must disappear to avoid my own imprisonment."

* * *

Garland Knight, once Edvin Karlsson, stormed out of the shed. Leaving the door flung open in his wake, he took large strides across the open ground to his car. After he entered the sedan, he drove up to the highway. He would put into action an escape plan that he and Victor Wong had worked out some years earlier. First, he would fly to Kraków, then go by car to the mountainous region of southern Poland, where a large home was well hidden in the forest about 500 feet above sea level. He would end his journey at one of the original and biggest of the houses for sex trafficking in Eastern Europe. The women held in that house came from Asia or Eastern Europe. Language differences kept these young women from interacting or making plans for anything beyond the life they now lived.

Once Edvin found his way to the house in Poland, he could have his pick of any girl in the bunch. He had left behind his wife and daughter without a second thought, but there was no reason to be lonely.

Not long after his arrival, a young lady from a broken home in Sweden was brought in, and she quickly caught his eye. Edvin decided to make her his management assistant. Within a few months, the two of them had grown close. They skied together on weekends, ate their meals together, and took frequent walks up the winding road into the mountains.

In the middle of his third winter in Poland, the weather forecast was for snow from early morning to midnight with short pauses. Although the day was frigid, Edvin was determined that he and Olga would go on their usual walk up the mountain. They started out hiking up the road, intending to turn around at the end of the first wave of snow, but the snow rapidly increased its intensity, swirling in their faces and blocking their vision home. The hour-long pauses predicted during the snowstorm never happened, and almost five feet of snow quickly accumulated on that side of the mountain.

The next week, higher temperatures melted most of the snow, and snowplows, which were gathered at a low point on the road, began their winding trip up the mountain. One of the trucks paused at a turn and then came to a complete stop. The driver exited slowly, trudging through the remnants of snow and ice to discover a blockage on the path—two frozen bodies clinging to each other.

* * *

After her father's discovery and quick exit from the shed, Aaron took Sara's hand, and the two of them rushed through the night back to the truck they had borrowed. When he turned on the headlights, he saw her face was streaked with tears. The truth about her father weighed heavily on her as she realized her entire life had been founded on a lie. He took her hand in his again and gazed into her eyes. All he could discern in those eyes now was sadness, disappointment, and betrayal. She might carry her father's genes, but her spirit was nothing like the man whose eyes exposed the vacant shadow of his soul.

As they sped through the night in a borrowed truck, Aaron knew what came next in her life wasn't likely to be pretty. Upheaval awaited her when the revelations about her father became public. He reached his right hand over to touch her arm, to offer a moment of reassurance. He would be there for whatever the future held.

The End